CANAAN CREEK

DAVID WOOTEN

SUNLAND PUBLISHING

Canaan Creek
Copyright © 2002 by David Wooten

ISBN 0-9718942-0-5

May 2002

Bible verses taken from the *King James Version*

Cover photo and author photo taken by Jake Egli

Printed in the Unites States of America

Sunland Publishing
P.O. Box 814
Bend, Oregon 97709

To my mother and father

1

The red and white spotted pony carrying Tommy Crawford hit the main street of Canaan Creek running full stride. It was early Sunday afternoon and the sun-soaked street lay empty except for a panting dog searching for some shade.

Tommy gripped the reins tight in his left hand, while he whipped with the right, guiding the pony past a blur of weathered facades. The weedy storefronts with broken glass and faded signs suggested Canaan Creek's best days remained somewhere in its not so recent past.

Barreling by the Onyx Saloon, Tommy glimpsed a man smoking a cigarette step out onto the boardwalk, his eyes squinting back the bright August sky. He regarded the boy with interest as he dashed by, and Tommy could feel a set of curious eyes following him all the way down the deserted street. It reminded Tommy that the Onyx used to be closed on the day of worship—a custom that changed soon after Jason Steele came to town.

Steele had surfaced in Canaan Creek the year before, but from where exactly, no one knew. It was common knowledge that he was enormously rich and surrounded himself with gunfighters of varying persuasions, although how he had accumulated his immense wealth remained a mystery.

Since his arrival into the Kern River Valley, which coincided conveniently with Canaan Creek's current drought, Steele had been actively buying up most of the surrounding ranches and land. All during a time when most ranchers found money in very short supply. Faced with the fear of losing everything that had taken a lifetime to obtain, many families sold out to Steele, and at prices most considered theft. In less than one year he now owned over half of the Kern River Valley.

Though his motives were certainly in question, his actions were legal. After all, Steele so pompously rationalized, "I'm at the very least giving these poor miserable souls something for their land, when there is a tremendous possibility they could lose everything and end up with nothing."

Steele was capitalizing on the misfortune of others and doing so in a haughty and callous manner. He did not endear himself at all to the people of the Kern River Valley, but that was neither his care nor concern. Jason Steele was a rich man and with his increasing wealth came more power. He could do anything he wanted, a fact he proved on numerous occasions, and because of his arsenal of trained gunmen he became feared. For that reason, when Jason Steele declared the Onyx Saloon would remain open on Sundays, no one cared to argue—or dared to.

Tommy raced on, his swift-footed pony leaving small puffs of red dirt in its wake. Up ahead the Canaan Creek Community Church shined as a beacon of white and a pillar of the town's former days. Resting peacefully at the north edge of town, the box-like structure sat directly in front of the now dry creek bed from which the town took its name. Three ponderosa pines stood guarding the small church; their long, shady branches spread out over the slanted roof like an angel's wings. While most of the other buildings in town were cracking and fading to a mixture of worn brown and gray, the three tall pines kept the Canaan Creek Community Church radiating as brilliant and white as the day it was built.

Tommy needed only a slight draw on the reins to bring his tired pony to a halt at the church's front steps. Bounding from the saddle, he could already hear the preacher's spirited voice booming from inside the open church doors:

"And my friends, I'm here to bear witness to you today, that the Devil's drought which holds this valley firmly in his grip, will come to an end! Just as the Good Lord in Heaven Above provided a miracle for the Children of Israel by opening up the Red Sea and drowning their would-be Egyptian captors, so will he provide a miracle for us here in Canaan Creek!"

No one in the small congregation hoped that would come true, or believed that it could, more than John McKinnley did. McKinnley sat stout in his familiar seat, third pew from the front, all the way to the far left-hand side. Strong, rugged, reverent, he was an impressive man on sight and the lines on his tan face spoke of experience rather than age. Rarely challenged, as few found reason to, he was well respected and admired for miles around. John McKinnley was a man tall in stature and wide in reputation.

McKinnley owned the Bar MC, a seventy-five thousand acre cattle ranch that encompassed some of the finest land in California. For more than ten years, McKinnley had been the largest landowner in the Kern River Valley— a distinction recently passed to Jason Steele. But Steele's prominence was dubious at best, for McKinnley's land nestled up against the base of the mountains where the Kern River flowed out from the High Sierra.

This gave McKinnley control of the free flow of water to every ranch in the Kern River Valley. It was a lofty position in the delicate time of a drought, and this standing allowed McKinnley some command over Steele. No matter how powerful Steele became, he could never gain complete reign over the valley that he so desperately lusted for without control of the water. Steele, of course, was well aware of this, as was McKinnley, and everyone in the valley watched and waited to see what would happen between the two.

The situation was volatile and McKinnley knew the problem was not about to go away. It was not in a man like Jason Steele to give up, and with his stable of professional gunmen, McKinnley wasn't so sure he could stop Steele from taking the Bar MC by force. A course of action Steele had hinted at only recently.

John McKinnley contemplated all of this during Preacher Jed Boyd's sermon, staring solemnly into his worn gray Stetson.

Sitting next to McKinnley was his daughter, Sarah.

Sarah McKinnley fixed herself straight and proper in the hard, uncomfortable pew, fanning herself as if all eyes were trained on her. Her flowing blonde hair, soft porcelain skin, and full lips were the fancy of most men in Canaan Creek, although few dared to approach her for fear of being shot down, not with a smoking gun, but with a stinging retort that most feared worse than any bullet.

Once, Sarah caught a daring cowboy stealing a peek at her from the pew in front, and she sent him reeling back around with an annoyed glare. It was not that Sarah didn't like being admired; actually she came to expect it, for she was well aware of her beauty and used it to her every advantage. No, it was that Sarah decided long ago what kind of man she wanted and this young cowboy didn't measure up.

Sarah was determined to move back East and marry a refined man. The kind who wore business suits, laundered and neatly pressed, rather than dusty old jeans and smelly wool shirts. She wanted a cosmopolitan man and make no mistake about it, Sarah always got what she wanted—if she didn't, there was hell to pay.

"Mr. McKinnley! Mr. McKinnley!" Tommy's piercing cry rang out from the back of the church.

"Young man, this is a place of worship!" Boyd rebuked from the pulpit.

"Sorry, Preach, but my Pa sent me."

McKinnley, out of his seat at the first shrill call of his name, joined the small boy at the back of the church.

"What is it, son?" McKinnley asked calmly, resting a hand on Tommy's bony shoulder.

"Some men are trying to blow up your dam!"

2

Gunfire echoed through the thin mountain air. Pepper Martin and Jack Crawford were exchanging bullets with two men they could not see. The two, believed to be Steele men, were concealed in a stand of cottonwood trees across the nearly dry Kern River bed.

Jack Crawford, McKinnley's neighbor and long-time friend, rose swiftly from behind the decaying trunk of a fallen pine he and Pepper were using for cover. He squeezed off a couple of rapid shots from his Henry rifle, and then, just as quickly, ducked back down. Sweat, from the blistering sun overhead and the adrenaline pumping fast through his veins, poured out from beneath Crawford's crusty hat and down the side of his red face.

"We can't keep 'em pinned down much longer," he said, promptly reloading. "This here's my last round."

It had been nearly an hour since Tommy rode away to get McKinnley and Crawford was becoming worried, not so much for himself and Pepper, but for his boy. Maybe something happened to Tommy on his way back to town. Pepper sensed Jack's growing concern. "He'll get here," he said.

Pepper Martin was McKinnley's foreman and his closest friend. He had served under McKinnley as a captain during the war, and once General Lee laid down his arms and surrendered his Confederate Army at Appomattox Court House, Pepper came West to help McKinnley build his dream ranch.

Now well into his sixties, Pepper's once brown hair was mostly gray. His body, though strong, was not quite as muscular, but he still carried himself like a man in his prime, only with a lifetime of experience to go with it. An avid reader and free thinker, Pepper kept most of what he knew and thought to himself, as a rule giving out opinions only when asked—and even then, reluctantly. But on those rare occasions when Pepper did choose to speak his mind, those present were inclined to listen. The three words he had just spoken made Jack Crawford feel instantly better.

Surveying the area, Pepper found their horses had moved down the mountain to get away from the noisy and erratic gunfire. The horses were a good fifty yards away and the land between uncovered by trees or brush. It was all open ground, and there would be no way to make a run for the horses without leaving themselves exposed to a potential bullet in the back. Their only chance, Pepper concluded, would be to hold out until McKinnley arrived.

"We'll just have to make these last rounds count," Pepper said.

The two Steele men across the riverbed were not hurting for ammunition. By the nature of their business they were used to finding themselves in situations such as this. Steele men carried bullets like beef to a barbecue. What the two men were doing on McKinnley land was not readily known, although Pepper and Crawford both suspected they were there to blow up the dam. Steele only days before had threatened to do just that, and the dam was less than three hundred yards up the riverbed from where Pepper and Crawford were now pinned down.

A crude structure made up of large pine logs and big round boulders, the dam was built with the help of all the ranchers in the valley, and its location on McKinnley land was chosen for many reasons, trust being foremost. All the valley's ranchers knew McKinnley would not cheat them out of water.

Steele opposed building the dam on McKinnley land from the very beginning. He trusted no man, as those who lack the quality rarely find it in themselves to trust others.

As the current drought continued with no apparent end in sight, worry gave way to distress. The drought permitted very little snow runoff coming out of the High Sierra, and it was taking nearly a month for the reservoir to refill back to full capacity. Cattle and sheep were dying in huge numbers, so the Kern River Valley Cattlemen's Association convened to come up with an alternate plan for water distribution.

The existing method of releasing water from the dam once it reached near capacity was not working. While it did replenish the dry creek beds downstream that forked off from the Kern River, it was determined that too much water was being lost or wasted in the process.

McKinnley suggested moving what was left of everyone's depleted herds to his land near the dam, thus bringing the cattle and sheep to the water, and eliminating the need for letting water out. The dam's reservoir would serve as one big watering hole.

These days the Kern River Valley consisted mostly of small ranches whose owners didn't raise cattle so much for profit, as they did for survival. With both McKinnley's and Steele's big herds gathered there it would certainly be crowded, and some cattle and sheep would still die off. But it was agreed that the plan might keep many of the ranchers from losing their entire herds—that is if the drought ended soon. If it didn't they could all go belly-up.

Everyone agreed to try McKinnley's plan . . . everyone except Steele.

Jason Steele flatly refused to move his cattle to McKinnley's land. Furthermore, he wanted his own water. The way Steele figured it, he owned most of the land and cattle; therefore, he was entitled to most of the water. Steele was of no mind to share with anyone and he demanded they come up with an alternate plan. McKinnley, backed by the vote of the other cattlemen, said, "*No!* We've all voted," he told Steele. "That's how it's going to be."

While it was true the ranchers were afraid of what Steele might do, there was some solace in the belief that safety sometimes comes in numbers. In the end, reality helped them overcome their fear. To give in to Steele would be to lose everything they had fought so hard to build.

Steele's refusal to go along with the other cattlemen was a power move on his part, and he lost. Steele was incensed. He had grown accustomed to getting his own way, and he stomped red-faced out of the meeting, threatening to blow up the dam if the vote wasn't changed.

Three days later two of his men were now caught riding out near that very same dam.

The Kern River bed was calm, the gunfire having ceased on both sides for several minutes. From behind the fallen tree, Pepper watched a blue jay glide by playfully overhead, calling out to another before it disappeared over the tops of the trees. The smell of gunpowder lingered in the air, and for the first time since the shots began Pepper realized how fiercely hot it was.

Across the riverbed, Logan Pfister strained his neck to listen. A thick man with a black mustache that hung into a frown, Pfister leaned his left shoulder heavily against the trunk of a tree, his .45 pointed skyward in his right hand.

"Hear that, Billy?" Pfister said.

The youngster with him appeared anxious and confused. "Hear what? I don't hear nothin'."

"That's what I'm talking about, you fool."

Pfister pushed off the tree and holstered his six-shooter. Billy, who was more boy than man having yet to experience his eighteenth birthday, appeared relieved. Sure he was capable if hired by Steele, but like most who try to make their way early in life with a gun, when push came to shove, they were usually looking for a respectable way out. This was his.

"Come on, let's get out of here," Billy said, springing from his crouch.

Pfister grabbed him by the collar. "Not so fast. Steele won't be happy if we come back without getting the job done." He let go of the boy's collar. "Besides, we're not letting those two old men off that easy. You stay here and make sure they don't try and make a run for it. I'm going to the horses and bring back some of that dynamite."

Billy didn't like it. "What about McKinnley? They sent that little kid for 'em."

"You let me worry about McKinnley." Pfister pointed across the riverbed. "You just make sure those two don't go nowhere."

Billy settled back onto his haunches, while Pfister turned toward the horses. The crisp cock of a rifle sent a chill through both of them.

It was John McKinnley standing tall, holding his Winchester belt-high and ready for action.

Logan Pfister stopped cold in his tracks. Meanwhile, his inexperienced young partner tried to spin from his crouch and fire off a shot.

McKinnley had anticipated the move and was ready. He fired once, knocking the six-shooter from Billy's grip, leaving a bloody flesh wound and a burning sting across his knuckles.

For a split-second Pfister thought of drawing, but in an instant McKinnley had his Winchester pulled back over, aiming into Pfister's belly. "Don't you be foolish, too," McKinnley warned.

Pfister's thought faded as quickly as it came.

"Now pull out that .45 . . . real slow . . . and let it fall," McKinnley ordered. A grin formed beneath Pfister's mustache. He knew he was beat, and so complied.

McKinnley, thumb resting on the hammer, pointed with the rifle at Billy. "You! Get over here."

The young gunman did as told, all the while trying to shake the pain from his bloody hand. "Ain't you a little young for this?" McKinnley commented. "What are you two doing on my land?"

"We wasn't doin' nothin'," Billy answered in a tone obviously not pleasing to McKinnley. "We was only passin' through when that foreman of yours got gun-happy."

McKinnley knew better. "With dynamite on those horses?" He shook his head in disgust. How much longer was this kind of thing to continue?

John McKinnley bore into the two gunmen with intense, threatening eyes. "I want you two to go back to your boss, and you tell him if he wants one drop of this water, he better bring those cattle of his up here himself. And you also tell him that if I ever catch another Steele man on my land again, I'm coming to deal with him *personally!* You understand that?"

Young Billy and Logan Pfister leaned back on their heels. McKinnley's overpowering presence did not allow them to answer.

"I said, do you understand?" This time they nodded. "Then let me hear you say it!"

"We understand."

"Good! Now get out of here! And I want to see you run to those horses."

McKinnley dropped the barrel of his Winchester. He watched as the two scrambled up an embankment, Billy struggling with his one good hand. When the sound of their horses faded, he called out to Pepper and Jack Crawford.

He was poking at the dirt with his boot toe, when both men came charging up.

"We heard a gunshot," Pepper called. "You, okay?"

"I'm all right," McKinnley answered, sounding both dismayed and disgusted.

Crawford peered around for the two men. "Where'd they go?"

"I sent them back to Steele with a message."

Crawford couldn't believe it. "You let 'em go?"

"This whole thing just ain't worth killing people over," McKinnley said. He paused, then added, "Nothing is."

"I don't know, John," Pepper spoke up. "If the lion doesn't kill the hunter, sooner or later, the hunter's gonna kill the lion."

McKinnley raised a graying eyebrow. Pepper had a point.

3

"For the last time, I am not going to sell this ranch."
John McKinnley's deep voice was full of resolve.

He was with his daughter Sarah on the balustraded
porch of their modest two-story ranch house. Behind them
the sun was about to set, outlining the jagged Sierra
peaks against a peaceful red sky. Night, like the seasons,
came slowly to the Kern River Valley, and while the
evening air was finally beginning to cool, the argument
between father and daughter was as hot as the day.

"You are so stubborn," Sarah replied.

Her father sighed. "Why can't you understand what I'm
telling you? If I sell this place to Steele, I'd be selling out
every rancher, every friend I have in this valley. Other
people's livelihoods are at stake here."

"Why is it you're always looking out for other people?"
Sarah questioned, before adding her own philosophy on

life. "Sometimes you have to look out for yourself, too, you know."

"I can't do that," McKinnley replied softly.

Sarah stepped forward, taking hold of her father's huge, gentle hands. She smiled warmly, trying to be as sincere as she could.

"Daddy, I want to go to school back East. I want to live where they have paved streets and use streetcars instead of horses. I want to live where people are civilized, and where they don't settle every argument with a gun. Is that so terrible? But I don't want you to sell this ranch just for me. I want you to sell it before something terrible happens . . . maybe to you."

"Nothing is going to happen to me," McKinnley answered sharply, pulling his hands free. "And I wish I could give you everything you want, I truly do. But with this drought, I simply don't have the money."

Though she tried to hide it, Sarah's rising anger began to show on her cross face. Up until now she had managed to control her emotions, not an easy thing for a person who wore her heart like an army officer's epaulet. With anyone else, Sarah wouldn't have cared about such a thing. She usually lashed out at anyone unwilling to let her have her way. This tactic did not work with her father and Sarah knew it. But now that it appeared she might be losing this battle—and to Sarah it was just that, a battle—she was not going down without a fight. Sarah knew what she was about to say would hurt her father, and she meant for it to.

"Adam asked me to marry him last night. If you can't send me to school, I'm afraid I'll have to say yes."

Adam! The mere mention of his name made McKinnley knit his brow.

Adam LeFloure was his Christian name and Sarah had run into him only five days before. It was on another of the valley's depressingly hot days and Sarah was bustling along the boardwalk at a rapid clip. She had been making the rounds of Canaan Creek while she waited for her father to finish up his business at the post office and the mercantile store.

Without warning, Adam stepped from the dusky doorway of the hotel restaurant directly in front of Sarah's path. She crashed into him like a runaway locomotive, and would have fallen if not for Adam's quick reaction and sure hands.

Sarah became angry and she slapped Adam's grip from around her waist, while attempting to regain her balance and composure. It wasn't until she was well into her stern lecture on the importance of "watching where one is going" that she looked at Adam and, more importantly, noticed how he was dressed.

Adam smiled at Sarah wearing a finely tailored broadcloth suit. His white silk shirt gleamed with pearl buttons from underneath a pinstriped coat, and his matching tie was knotted with perfection around his neck.

There was no disputing that Adam was from the East, and that alone made Sarah fall for him instantly. It was only later that she would behold his polite manner, courteous smile, and warm brown eyes that seemed to draw Sarah in and carry her away. As far as Sarah was concerned, all that was more pudding for the pie.

Few Easterners made their way through Canaan Creek, so she considered their chance meeting somewhat fateful—although Sarah did not usually believe in such things as faith or miracles.

Sarah learned that Adam was in Canaan Creek only because he had failed to make it back to the stage on time. When he stepped off the stage to get something to eat, the driver assured him it would be at least an hour before they would be leaving. The team of horses needed to be fed and watered. When Adam returned forty-five minutes later the stage was gone, headed speedily towards Bakersfield where Adam was to catch a train to San Francisco.

He planned to continue his journey by taking the next stage three days later, but now a week had passed and Adam was still in Canaan Creek.

"You just met him!" Sarah's father protested. "How could you possibly marry him? You don't know anything about him."

"I know he'll take me back East with him," Sarah remarked sarcastically. "That's all I need to know."

"Why are you doing this?"

"I'm seventeen years old, Daddy—I don't want to grow old out here. And I don't want to watch this ranch get taken away from you."

"Jason Steele will never get this ranch," McKinnley said irritably.

"How are you going to stop him? Steele's got close to thirty men. All we have is Pepper, and maybe Mr. Crawford. No one else around here will stand up against Steele."

McKinnley frowned. He knew the odds all too well. "The Lord will provide a way," he said.

"I don't know if I would count on that."

In an instant her father's face went flush. John McKinnley was a God-fearing man who regarded his faith seriously and he expected, he demanded, his only daughter do the same. McKinnley found Sarah's remark downright disrespectful, bordering on blasphemy.

"I don't ever want to hear that kind of talk from you again, young lady!" McKinnley said sternly. "And as for sending you to school, I just don't have the money."

"Then I guess I'm going to have to marry Adam," Sarah bawled. She stomped off into the house, slamming the big oak door behind her.

4

The flaming red sky of sunset faded, overtaken by a clean slate of purple that slowly gave way to the silver and black of night. The smell of pine scented the air and chirping crickets, along with a host of winged insects, came out to play. This was John McKinnley's favorite time of day, and he would often spend it sitting on the front porch with Pepper after the day's work had been done. They would relax in the cool evening air, talking about the ranch, discussing current events, or reminiscing about their days together in the war.

Pepper didn't join McKinnley on this evening, he knew his friend needed to be alone.

John McKinnley leaned back in a chair; the heels of his black boots propped up on the oak balustrade. His argument with Sarah played heavily on his mind. Reflectively he worked a pipe, its smoke curling up around him in a fine, sweet-smelling mist. As darkness settled in, McKinnley's thoughts slowly drifted off to his father . . .

Robert McKinnley was a tall man like his son, but much thinner, being sick with consumption throughout most of his adult life. McKinnley's father coughed, hacked, and wheezed uncontrollably. He endured a distressing time trying to sleep, and as a result had very little stamina. Young John would often cry himself into the sleep his father could not have, listening to him struggle. As a small boy, McKinnley was consumed with helplessness knowing there was nothing he could do to help his ailing father.

When John McKinnley reached his early teens, the American West was only beginning to come into its own as a romanticized, endless frontier. There was unlimited land and boundless opportunity, all for the taking. A land flowing with milk and honey. McKinnley never tired of listening to the men who'd returned from the West talk about and tell stories of their adventures there. As a budding young man, John McKinnley dreamed of seeing and experiencing this *Promise Land* for himself. But when he was finally old enough to go, he couldn't bring himself to leave his frail and weak father to pursue his foolish, childhood dreams.

McKinnley tried at length to talk his father into moving out West. Many a doctor told Robert McKinnley the arid climate would benefit his health, maybe even add a few years to his life. But John's father wouldn't hear of it. Robert McKinnley had lived his whole life in Ohio and that's where they were going to bury him. He always joked, "When it's my time, I don't want God to have to look hard to find me."

If not for the Civil War, John McKinnley might never have left his father or their small Ohio town. And when he did leave, McKinnley felt deep in his heart that he would probably never see his father alive again. He did not know the same would bear true for his mother.

Robert McKinnley finally succumbed to the disease he so bravely fought less than six months after his son left to fight for the Union Army. John's mother, Sarah, emotionally drained from the long years of caring for her sick husband and now left with an unfillable void, soon joined him.

If there was any comfort for McKinnley in the war it was that it left little time for grieving, and with so much death surrounding him, it was somewhat easier for him to accept the passing of his beloved parents. When the war ended, McKinnley, with no home to return to, headed West. To this day he had never gone back to Ohio.

A pleasant breeze made its way through the dry pines. McKinnley got up, stretched, repacked his pipe. A silver moon illuminated the Greenhorn Mountains to the south. It was the same three-quarter moon he and his father talked under the night before McKinnley left for war.

That evening father and son talked at great length about life, death, and God. There were no tears or unspoken regrets, only true, honest feelings shared by two men under a warm autumn sky. It was that night McKinnley received his most treasured possession: his father's *King James Bible*. The same Bible Robert's father had given him.

The old book was black and heavy, and in great condition, for its previous owners handled it with extreme care and reverence. The leather covering, worn smooth from years of use, protected its yellowing pages, frayed at the edges from extensive reading and study. McKinnley recalled many an evening in front of a fire, listening to his father read from its pages the stories of Moses, Abraham, and Christ.

John's father worked the pages with quivering fingers. "This book right here is what gave me the strength and courage to keep going," he told his son. "If not for this book, I would have died long ago."

Robert McKinnley began to read from *Exodus 23:20:*

"Behold, I send an Angel before thee, to keep thee in the way, and to bring you into the place which I have prepared.

"Beware of him, and obey his voice, provoke him not; for he will not pardon your transgressions; for my name is in him.

"But if thou shalt indeed obey his voice, and do all that I speak; then I will be an enemy unto thine enemies, and an adversary unto thine adversaries."

When he finished, Robert McKinnley carefully closed the Bible and handed it to his son. He said, "Son, I don't know why the Lord chooses to do what he does. I don't know why he gave me this illness. Maybe I was chosen as a kind of sacrifice for someone else, so they could go on and achieve and contribute to the good of all in ways I would never have been capable." Robert McKinnley licked his lips, choosing his words carefully.

"What I'm telling you, son, is that it's not important for us to know why God lets certain things happen. It's more important to realize, and to know, that He's right there with you while it's happening. Remember that when you're out there all alone fighting that war."

With that, Robert McKinnley struggled to his feet and shuffled inside. It was the last time McKinnley saw his father alive.

"You gonna stay out here all night?" It was Pepper and his words cut into McKinnley's memory, bringing him back to the moment.

McKinnley rubbed a palm into his tired eyes. He had no idea how long he'd been sitting out on the porch, but he figured it must have been well over an hour since the moon was now tucked out of view behind the Greenhorns.

He tapped out the remains of his pipe on the porch rail, taking time to reform his thoughts. "Pepper," he finally said, "I'm closing out our account tomorrow at the bank."

Pepper shook his head. He had heard part of the father-daughter argument earlier from inside the house. "Because of Sarah? You can't do that!" Pepper knew McKinnley could do with his money as he pleased, but McKinnley had always referred to the ranch as *ours*, not just his. It was this kind of unselfishness that made Pepper proud to serve under him, and work for him.

"I ain't got no choice," McKinnley reasoned. "I can't let her go off half-cocked and marry some man she's known less than a week because she's mad at me."

Pepper, who'd been standing halfway out the front door, stepped onto the porch, closing the door behind him. "Well, if you ask me, I think you should turn her over your knee and knock some sense into her."

McKinnley grinned. "A few years ago I probably would have done just that, but she's not a little girl anymore.

She's got her dreams just like I did when I was her age, and I figure, being her father, I should give her a chance at 'em."

"But we . . . *you* can't afford it right now."

"Pepper, if this drought don't end soon, I never will."

5

Earl Wallace was a portly gentleman with rose colored cheeks. He wore an ill-fitting brown suit and stood hunched over a desk counting out money—John McKinnley's money. Wallace was President of the Kern River Valley Bank and McKinnley watched him with pained interest from the other side of the desk.

The bills, mostly hundred-dollar bank notes, were all crisp and new, and each smacked with freshness as they left the banker's stubby hands.

"Eighteen hundred dollars and thirty-seven cents," Wallace finally announced, putting down the last hundred along with its change. "That's all of it." The banker backed away, saddened. He had done this a lot lately and he didn't like it. "I'm sorry to see you doing this, John. You've had an account here for over fifteen years."

McKinnley reached down and picked up the money. "And I will again," he stated with certainty.

The morning sun was only beginning to rise over the tops of the facades and already it was hot. It was early, just past eight o'clock, and the long shadows on the waking street were beginning their gradual withdrawal. John McKinnley exited the bank, his money tucked safely away in an envelope in his shirt pocket.

Out on the street, a man in a wagon rattled by giving McKinnley a friendly wave as he passed. Across the street, two men idled outside the Onyx. McKinnley paused for a moment taking in the fresh morning air. He could hear tiny feet on the boardwalk and he turned to see a young red-haired girl approaching, her freckled red arms folded with books on her way to school.

He tipped his hat in greeting and the young girl answered with a wide and blushing grin. McKinnley watched her until she disappeared around the corner, then he stepped down to the street where his appaloosa patiently waited at the hitch-rail.

McKinnley gave the gray spotted horse an affectionate slap and began to tighten the cinch on its saddle. He wasn't worried about the cinch being loose; rather he was using the time to casually observe the two men he had noticed moments before outside the saloon. Their hard, unprincipled look gave them away as Steele men, and McKinnley knew their loitering outside the Onyx was not by chance. McKinnley was constantly being watched, and word of every place he went and every person he talked to eventually made its way back to Jason Steele.

Done with the saddle, McKinnley ceremoniously pulled out his Winchester from its scabbard. He had always preferred a rifle to a handgun and he made a big show of inspecting it, making sure that the two men could see that it was loaded and ready. If they wanted to find out what he carried from the bank, they were going to have to pay a high price for it. Finished, McKinnley shoved the Winchester back into the scabbard and swung into the saddle. The appaloosa, happy to be moving again, jumped out into a trot.

"Mr. McKinnley!" The call came from behind.

The anxious voice belonged to a short man in suspenders who wore the blurry-eyed appearance of overwork. The man rushed out to meet McKinnley, who had snapped the appaloosa back around.

"I have a telegram for you," the man said, nearly out of breath. He held the folded note up to the big man in the saddle. "Another came in as you were leaving the bank. I was afraid I'd missed you."

McKinnley steadied the appaloosa so he could read:

> *In regards to the incident in Mojave in which your daughter Sarah was involved: Be informed that she has been officially cleared of any wrongdoing.*
>
> *Tom Chapman*
> *New Sheriff, Mojave*

It was obvious that McKinnley was pleased. "Good news, huh?" The messenger said.

McKinnley folded up the telegram. "I'll say. This is the first piece of good news I've had in quite a spell."

The Bar MC was an hour's ride west of Canaan Creek, through a land dotted with pine trees, juniper, cypress, and at the lower elevations, oak and an occasional Joshua tree. The tall peaks of the Sierra shadowed the rider and at the base of the small rocky hills that lined the valley floor, huge boulders sat clustered and silent. The giant rocks served as a reminder of how strong a force the Kern River had once been, when it carved out the valley millions of years before. That very same river was now reduced to little more than a trickle.

John McKinnley cut across the brown meadows; a solitary figure moving against a fixed, dying world. The sun beat down behind him, but the breeze brought on by the appaloosa's canter made him feel good in the saddle. McKinnley never did mind the ride to and from town, and he especially enjoyed it when he was alone. He would use the time to contemplate business, recite old poems or clear his mind, and lately he had spent most of his time on the latter.

McKinnley wasn't convinced he was doing the right thing by closing out his account at the bank. He felt he was making a hasty decision, spurred by Sarah's threat of getting married. He did not like acting on impulse. He preferred taking time to think things out carefully, instead of using emotion as his guiding light. But it wasn't as though he hadn't agonized over his decision. He hardly slept the night before and he continued to work it over in his mind earlier that morning on the ride in to town. Every way McKinnley considered it, he found himself coming back to the same conclusion: he couldn't bring himself to allow Sarah to run off and get married because she was mad at him.

And what about this man she was to marry . . . this Adam LeFloure. Who was he, really? He was from back

East, that much McKinnley knew, but from where exactly? Adam said he was on his way to San Francisco on business when he stepped off the stage, but what kind of business was he involved with? McKinnley didn't know and Sarah, he suspected, didn't know either. And why was Adam traveling through Canaan Creek to get to San Francisco? If he was, indeed, coming from the East as he had said, Canaan Creek certainly was not the most direct route.

Too many things about this Adam didn't add up in McKinnley's mind. Besides, there was something about the man himself that rubbed McKinnley the wrong way, although what it was exactly, he couldn't say. The two men were introduced once during Adam's brief sojourn into the valley, and on that occasion the two got along well enough to even share a laugh. Nothing McKinnley had seen or heard gave him reason to suspect Adam was anything other than what he appeared to be: a charming, polite, educated, well-spoken man. *But still . . .*

McKinnley shook his head at himself and broke into a smile. He recognized that he would probably be suspect of any man who wanted to marry his daughter. This did not mean he approved of Sarah marrying Adam. John McKinnley did not believe any person should marry someone they had known less than a month of Sundays— even though he knew he was going to marry Sarah's mother the first night they met at the annual Fourth of July barbecue. Things were different, McKinnley reasoned, back in his day.

Up ahead, McKinnley could now see Lizard Rock, an ancient boulder formation resembling the head of a large reptile. It jutted out from a mound of boulders, which marked the approach of McKinnley's land. On the other side of Lizard Rock sat the French Gulch Bridge. Once McKinnley crossed the wooden suspension bridge he would be on his land and almost home.

McKinnley had built the French Gulch Bridge many years before to cut down the trip from the Bar MC to Canaan Creek by almost half. The only other way to get to the Bar MC equally as fast would be to cut across Cane Break Meadow, and then come directly up the south fork of the Kern River. Now, with the riverbed almost dry, that was not a problem, but when it was filled with rushing water it was an extremely hard and dangerous ride, especially for the horses that could easily break a leg slipping on the rocky bottom below.

Eager to get home, McKinnley eased the appaloosa into a gallop. He had picked up a current newspaper before leaving town, and he couldn't wait to read that paper and get out of this miserable heat.

Rounding Lizard Rock, the French Gulch Bridge came slowly into view . . . and so did the four riders blocking the road.

6

John McKinnley reined in directly in front of the four riders. He recognized them immediately and he made a point of pulling his appaloosa in close, letting the men know if anyone was going to back down, it wasn't going to be him. Straight across from him, sitting smug on a black stallion, was Jason Steele.

Steele lounged casually in his saddle, wearing an insolent grin that seemed permanently fixed on his pockmarked face. He was not a big man—in boots he was barely five and a half feet tall—but what he lacked in physical size he made up for with hired guns. Jason Steele was a cold, calculating man who cared little for others, and that included his own men. But these same men were well compensated for their servitude, and that meant more to the kind of man Steele hired than how they were treated by the boss. Three of these men now flanked Steele, blocking the French Gulch Bridge and McKinnley's way home. A very large, heavy-set man was on Steele's immediate left. The man's double-chinned face was badly sunburned and he wore his wide-brimmed hat pulled down low over his eyes to prevent further damage from the sun. A shaggy black beard hung from his chin, and the only time McKinnley got a good glimpse of the man's face was when he raised his head to spit out his chew.

On the other side of Steele sat Joe Dunbar. Dunbar was Steele's foreman and right-hand man. A lean figure with menacing, cat-like eyes, Joe carried himself with a deadly cockiness that he backed up with a fast draw. Only two weeks before, McKinnley himself watched Joe gun-down two of his own men outside the Onyx. The two had made the mistake of challenging Joe's authority and ended up paying for it with their lives. McKinnley watched the first man go down before he could even make a play for his gun. The second managed to barely get the barrel of his six-shooter showing before he received three lethal slugs in the chest. Joe made it appear effortless, and then proclaimed that if anyone else wanted to dispute his authority, they had "better not make plans for supper."

Sitting on Joe's left was the boy, Billy, whom McKinnley had encountered at the riverbed the day before. Billy's right hand was heavily bandaged and McKinnley noted the boy appeared nervous.

"Didn't get your fill yesterday?" McKinnley said to him.

Billy didn't answer, attempting instead to avoid McKinnley's piercing glare.

"Good morning, John," Steele greeted, his voice rich with sarcasm. "You're out early today."

"Had some business to attend to," McKinnley answered dryly.

"At the bank, I understand."

"Word travels fast."

Steele shifted in the saddle and McKinnley wondered if Steele was attempting to make himself appear taller. "We were headed out your way. Why don't we ride together, so we can talk."

"No—I like to ride alone. Besides, we ain't got nothing to talk about."

"I disagree, John," Steele replied. "Why I believe we have a great deal to talk about. I'm still entertaining the idea of buying your ranch."

"It's not for sale!" McKinnley replied irritably. He jerked on the reins and the appaloosa jumped out to the right, but the fat man immediately slid out his mount, preventing McKinnley from passing.

"Don't you at least want to hear my offer?"

McKinnley's senses were now on full alert. He became suddenly aware of the warmth of the sun on his back, the jingle of spurs in the stirrup, and the creak and smell of saddle leather. He knew he was in trouble. There was no way he could handle all four men by himself. Regardless, he wasn't about to back down.

"You don't listen very good, do you, Steele? I told you, my ranch ain't for sale. And even if it was, I would never sell it to you." McKinnley's icy glare moved to the big man blocking him. "Now tell your fat man there to get that mule he's on out of the way, or I'm going to shoot it out from under him."

The fat man's face shot up and Joe and Billy came to life in their saddles.

Steele ignored the threat. "I understand your daughter ran into a little trouble a few months back in Mojave. I hear the sheriff there would . . . how should we say it . . . look forward to seeing her again."

It was obvious that Steele was not aware of the telegram McKinnley carried with him. But how, McKinnley wondered, did Steele find out about the incident in Mojave? Only three people were supposed to know: Sarah, Pepper, and himself, and they certainly were not talking.

McKinnley pulled the appaloosa back in front of Steele. "What's your point?"

"Point is, you sell me your ranch and I won't tell the sheriff of Mojave where he can find your daughter."

"You go to hell!" McKinnley thundered.

The big horse leapt out at McKinnley's kick, but almost instantaneously reared back, for its rider had jerked back hard on the reins. The appaloosa kicked with its front legs high in the air. It let out a frightened neigh, and when the excited horse's front hoofs touched back down, McKinnley fell off the backside, his chest having been pierced by two bullets from Joe's .45.

Under the clear summer sky, John McKinnley lay face down in the dirt . . . *dead*.

Steele and his men steadied their mounts after the quick and one-sided gun-battle.

"I thought he was going for his gun," Joe exclaimed, pumped up with the adrenaline of killing. Joe was not one to apologize for a shooting, but he knew this one, like no other, held special significance.

"It's all right, Joe," Steele replied, eerily calm. "He was going to have to die sooner or later, might as well have been now." After a moment of consideration, Steele looked over at Billy whose eyes were as big as silver dollars. "See what he's got on him."

Billy jumped down, uneasy about what he had just witnessed. Tentatively, he rolled McKinnley's body over with his boot.

John McKinnley's face was soiled with dirt and fresh blood trickled out of the corner of his mouth. Billy's heart was beating so fast, he was afraid that Steele and the others could hear it—to him it was deafening.

Inside McKinnley's shirt pocket he found the envelope containing the money. "Hey, lookie' here!" Billy shouted, excited with his find. He fanned out the bank notes like a deck of cards.

Joe and the fat man leaned down for a closer look. "How much you figure's there?" the fat man asked, before spitting some chew.

Billy's excitement grew with each hundred he counted. "Looks like over a thousand dollars, near's I can tell." He handed up the money to Steele and all four broke into a defiant laughter.

Billy found the telegram next.

"What's that?" Joe asked.

Billy handed it up to Joe. "Looks like a note or somethin'."

Joe didn't reach for it. "Why don't you read it to us?"

A self-conscious smile broke out on Billy's boyish face. "I was gonna check his other pockets."

"You already did," Joe replied, his tone becoming harsh, "I was watching."

The two stared at each other in uncomfortable silence. After a moment, Billy glanced at Steele and then to the fat man for solace . . . none was offered.

Joe became impatient. "I ain't gonna tell you again—read it!"

Billy's lips tightened. "I can't read!" he finally blurted, embarrassment replacing his anger.

Joe mocked him with a laugh, joined by the fat man. The boy's shameful admission amused even Steele. Billy clenched his teeth and hate poured into his eyes. The thought of drawing his .45 flashed into his mind. Billy's right hand was bandaged, but Joe knew the young gunman was equally adept with his left—it was one of the reasons Steele hired him.

"If you think you're fast enough, you go right ahead and try it," Joe challenged him.

Billy knew that to draw would be to die. He wanted to let the moment pass, but Joe wasn't so inclined.

"Come on, you know you're itchin' to," Joe goaded him.

"Knock it off, Joe," Steele cut in. "I can't have you killing off all my men." He threw down one of his gloved hands. "Give me that paper!"

Steele began to read. Meanwhile, Billy climbed sheepishly back into the saddle, Joe's eyes stalking him.

When Steele finished, he was intrigued. "Well, it appears as though John was one up on me." He tore up the telegram, letting the pieces rain down on McKinnley's lifeless body. "No, John, you go to hell."

Steele whirled his stallion. "Come on, let's get out of here!" He kicked the stallion into a gallop and they were off, whooping and hollering into the distance.

When the shouts subsided and the four riders were out of sight, a man appeared from the nearby trees.

7

The man from the trees attracted a great deal of attention as he ambled up the main street of Canaan Creek. The blazing sun lit a path before him, while trailing behind was McKinnley's solemn appaloosa, its owner draped unceremoniously across its saddle.

The man was a striking figure, high atop an impressive red roan that moved in an easy, deliberate style befitting its rider. The brim of his hat cast a shadow across his face, hiding his capable eyes from view.

The man appeared to be a dangerous force in the openness of the street, but his outward semblance was in complete contrast to his countenance; for around his waist he wore no gun and in his scabbard he carried no rifle. Yet he appeared to be a man who could use both, and well, without the need to prove it.

Whoever this man was, he was being extremely showy with his parade through the center of town, and it was obvious that he meant to be. Only those with secrets keep to the back roads and alleyways, and it was readily apparent this man felt he had nothing to hide.

He led his roan to the front hitch of the sheriff's office and slid casually from the saddle. Sheriff Dan MacLean was cleaning a six-shooter at his desk when the man entered.

"You the sheriff?" he asked casually.

"That's what the badge says," MacLean answered, not bothering to look up. "I suppose there's a reason you're in here to bother me."

"I want to report a murder."

MacLean lifted an aloof eye from the polished pistol. He didn't recognize the man standing before him, and that made the sheriff uncomfortable. MacLean was not a sheriff in the true sense of the word; rather another pawn in Steele's deadly game.

The previous sheriff, an honest family man by the name of Ed Marsh, had been murdered seven months before by another member of Steele's legion. A fabricated story was thrust upon the townspeople and while few believed it, none, with the exception of John McKinnley, were willing to call Steele on it. Steele had the town scared, and most believed that if he would go so far as to have the sheriff murdered, he certainly wouldn't hesitate to kill one of them to make sure he got away with it. McKinnley could do nothing more than watch while Steele appointed MacLean the new sheriff, unchallenged.

"Murder?" MacLean said. "Just who do you say was murdered?"

"John McKinnley."

The stranger now had the sheriff's undivided attention. Outside, news of McKinnley's death spread through Canaan Creek like wildfire. The street was filling with people, and a short distance from McKinnley's limp body a swarm of onlookers stood camped, speculating. Upon leaving his office, MacLean recognized McKinnley's appaloosa right off and a nervous twinge began to grow in the sheriff's stomach. MacLean knew the rest would be a formality.

"All right you people, stand back!" MacLean ordered, as if to declare his presence and validity.

The throng surged back and the sheriff went reluctantly about his duty. It was clear he was not enjoying this, and after much hesitation, he pulled the body's dangling head up by the hair.

"That's McKinnley, all right," MacLean confirmed uneasily. The pang in his stomach grew tighter. "How do you know it was murder?" he said, turning to the stranger.

"I was there when it happened." A slow murmur ran through the crowd. "I was in the trees," the man added.

Sheriff MacLean jerked the man away from the interested flock. He didn't want anyone to hear what this man might say. "Then you must have seen who done it."

"Jason Steele and three of his men."

MacLean wrinkled his forehead. "That's a very dangerous accusation to be making around here, mister," MacLean told him in low tones. "Where you from?"

"Nowhere in particular."

"You got a name?"

"Keene."

"Well, Keene," MacLean started in severely, "I suggest you get back up there on that big horse of yours and you ride on to wherever it is you come from. Because you're not going to be alive very long here in Canaan Creek, throwing around accusations like the one you just made."

"Sheriff, I saw what I saw."

MacLean looked him over hard. The man in front of him appeared sure of himself without a hint of cockiness. Finally MacLean said, "How do I know you didn't kill him?"

Keene smiled. "Not even you believe that, sheriff. You know I wouldn't have brought him in if I had. I take this to mean you're not going to at least check out my story?"

"You let me worry about my job," MacLean barked. "And if I was you, I'd take my advice."

All through the hot afternoon, people flooded the streets of Canaan Creek with talk of McKinnley's murder and the man who brought him in to town. A morbid excitement was settling in—the kind that only death can bring—and with each passing hour, the story of John McKinnley's murder was changed and twisted as it passed from person to person like a piece of Holy Bread. By nightfall even the truth would sound like a lie.

Sheriff Dan MacLean stepped from the cramped confines of the undertaker's office and started for his own office down the street. It was nearly three o'clock and the sun was on its downward slide toward the Greenhorn peaks. MacLean was tired. Usually he would be napping about now. Crossing the street, the sheriff could feel the eyes of the town upon him and it made him uncomfortable. A man could get away with more when he wasn't being watched. For MacLean, the walk across the street might well have been a walk across the valley.

Reaching the door of his office, the sheriff was looking forward to a clean swallow of the whiskey he had tucked away in the bottom drawer of his desk. He would need it for the ride out to Steele's which was to follow. Pushing inside, the sheriff found that ride no longer necessary. Sitting on the corner of his desk was Jason Steele.

"I was coming out to see you," MacLean said, somewhat unsettled by Steele's presence. He glanced hesitantly over at Joe Dunbar, who was viewing the street through the green cloth curtains in the corner.

"I understand someone brought in McKinnley," Steele said.

"He was in the trees," MacLean informed him. "Couldn't you at least of been a little more discreet?"

"What are you going to do, sheriff," Steele remarked sarcastically, "lock us up?"

MacLean fumbled for an answer, but Steele cut him off. "Oh relax, sheriff. You're taking your job way too seriously." Steele got up and peeked through the curtains alongside Joe. "Where is this person now who hides in trees?"

"I saw him go into the saloon about an hour ago."

Steele turned to Joe, who left without saying a word.

The man who brought in McKinnley faced the long bar of the Onyx, his back to the room. The saloon was loud and crowded with mostly Steele men bunched in large groups around tables and at the bar. There was only one topic on this hot afternoon, and in the mirror behind the bar the man could see himself being talked about and pointed out to each newcomer who entered. None of these men knew that he had fingered their boss for McKinnley's murder. If they had, he would have already found trouble.

Joe flung open the bat-wing doors of the Onyx and strode purposefully inside. He stopped at a nearby table of Steele men, who indicated for him the stranger at the bar. Joe's entrance did not go unnoticed by Keene. His eyes were on Joe in the mirror from the moment he stepped through the swinging doors.

Joe strutted up to the bar, his expression hostile. He half-circled the stranger, sizing him up like a lion stalking its prey. He noticed right off the man carried no gun—and was disappointed.

"How come you don't wear no gun?" Joe snarled, crowding in close.

"Only reason to carry a gun is to kill someone," Keene replied casually. "I don't plan on doing that."

"What if they're plannin' to kill you?"

Keene inspected his beer, ignoring Joe's fierce glare. "You looking to gun me down in cold blood, like you did McKinnley?" He said it easily, but loud enough to be heard throughout the saloon. It was as good as a slap in the face. The Onyx fell silent and all eyes went to Joe for a reaction.

Joe swelled with anger, and as was usually the case when he became enraged, his gun soon followed. Joe drew up his Colt in a fury, sending the men behind Keene scrambling to get out of the potential line of fire.

"You're stickin' your nose where it don't belong, mister," Joe warned.

The man before him did not flinch, tremble, or blink. He continued only to look straight ahead, acting as though Joe was more of an annoyance than a threat.

This served to fuel Joe's fire even more. Failure to get a response after he drew his gun had never happened to Joe. Consequently, he wasn't sure what to do next. Joe held the gun, but he didn't feel he had the advantage, and like most uneducated men who live behind the fast draw of a gun, it is the weapon itself that does their talking. When this fails them they are left to look foolish, having no other recourse of action. Fortunately for Joe, he was wearing another option low on his left hip.

Joe drew up his other .45 and slammed it down on the bar. "Pick it up," he demanded. The invitation was now out.

Keene's poised eyes dropped down sideways, casually taking in the pearl handled Russian Colt. His face seemed to cloud with a look of regretful pain, as if he was about to be forced to do something against his will, not out of fear, but out of regret.

Joe was restless. "I said, pick it up!"

Keene's attention went back to his beer. "You're getting impatient, Joe. That's a dangerous thing to be when you're gunning for a man."

"Shut up and pick up that .45!"

Keene smiled, catching Joe's eyes in the mirror. "You don't want me to do that, Joe. Remember, I've seen you draw."

"Look mister, you're not gonna talk your way out of this, so pick up that piece and let's get to business."

For the first time, Keene turned and faced Joe directly. "Joe, you just don't get it, do you? You strut all around, barking out orders, expecting everyone to jump out of fear of being gunned down. Well, I got news for you, Joe. You don't frighten me—you annoy me. I've seen your kind a thousand times before. That fast draw of yours makes you feel like a big man, makes you feel important.

"Trouble is, it's not forever. You see, Joe, no matter how quick you are with that .45, there's always someone out there who's a little bit faster. And sooner or later, they cross your path. Remember what the Good Book says, Joe: *Those who take the sword, perish by the sword.*"

For a moment Joe was taken in by the man's words. He rubbed his three-day growth of beard, then tipped his hat back and grinned. Deep down, there was actually a part of this man he admired. "Well now, I never figured you for no Bible thumper." Joe turned and faced his men. "Check it out, boys. We got us a Preacher Boy amongst us, and he thinks quotin' the Bible's gonna save him."

A mocking roar of laughter went up through the saloon. Joe felt like his old self again. His grin disappeared and he was serious.

"All right, Preacher Boy, I'm not gonna tell you again. Pick up that gun or I'll shoot you where you stand."

Keene refused. "No, Joe, I don't want to kill you," and he turned and started for the door.

Joe's lanky arm reached out and grabbed Keene by the shoulder. He spun him around and sent his gun crashing down across the side of Keene's jaw. It was a vicious blow, and Keene went toppling over a card table, scattering a group of Steele men.

Joe stepped to Keene, shoving the busted table out of the way. "You didn't think you was just gonna walk on outta' here, did you? If you don't want to do it with guns, we can—"

Keene's boot came up catching Joe squarely in the groin. Joe buckled instantly in pain and fell to the sawdust-covered floor.

Keene worked himself to his feet. "Trouble with you is, Joe, you talk too much."

Standing over Joe, Keene brushed the back of his hand across his bloody jaw, glancing at the hard faces surrounding him. Most of these were Joe's men, but there wasn't one among them who, deep down, felt sorry to see Joe doubled over in pain. Keene cleaned his bloody hand on his pant leg, and when it was evident none of the men around him were willing to take up the fight for Joe head-on, he stepped towards the door.

Joe let out a yell! He leaped to his feet and rushed Keene, tackling him. As Keene pushed up from the floor, three of Joe's men grabbed him, giving Joe time to get to his feet. They pinned Keene's arms behind him, then hauled him up and held him.

"I told you, you wasn't gonna walk out of here," Joe said. Then he spit in Keene's face and began to slam his fists repeatedly into Keene's stomach. At first, Keene's body was able to withstand the assault from Joe's punches. But slowly, Keene began to weaken and his tough body grew soft. When he could stand no more, Joe's men let him fall to the floor. That's when Joe began to kick Keene; first in the groin; then in the stomach; then in the face. At some point Keene lost consciousness. "Put him out in the street," Joe instructed.

His men picked up Keene and tossed him out through the bat-wing doors.

The entire saloon poured outside. Keene was in the dirt on his back, semiconscious. Blood covered him and his face was so badly cut and swollen, it hardly resembled that of a man.

Joe pushed his way through the crowd, pleased. Again, he had proven himself in front of his men—even if he needed help—and he felt good.

He stomped on Keene's hand and kicked him in the side. "Preacher Boy," he said, "I don't want to ever see you again. Cause next time I do I'm gonna kill you, gun or no gun!"

And he kicked him again.

8

The sun beat down on the valley floor, baking the grass and turning the once inviting green land into an infertile, gray landscape. The Kern River Valley canyons were quiet and nothing moved across its brown meadows or in the empty blue sky. It had been two days since John McKinnley's death.

It came as no surprise that nearly every person within fifty miles would turn out for McKinnley's funeral. And just as he would have wanted it, there were no words spoken in his honor; no speeches made extolling his virtues. It was a brief, simple service, and there was not one dry eye in the crowd.

John McKinnley was buried in his blue Sunday suit, his once brawny arms folded across his Stetson. Until the wooden casket was being lowered into the grave Sarah had managed to hold back her tears. But as her father disappeared under a mound of dirt the weight of what was happening finally hit her—like a mule's kick, it nearly knocked her over. She was burying her father, and if she ever had any, her faith, too. Sarah couldn't comprehend how God could let a man like her father be killed when he had put his entire life and trust in His hands. As far as Sarah was concerned, her father had lived his life for something that didn't exist. He had died in vain, living for something that was never there.

John and Elizabeth McKinnley's graves were side by side. Husband and wife were reunited in the shade of a two-hundred-year-old oak tree. It was to this very spot that McKinnley and his young bride had come often in the days before her untimely death. From beneath the native oak's comforting branches, the entire Kern River Valley could be taken in from one end to the other. It was a rich valley then; budding with wildlife, green grass, and a roaring Kern River filled with big, colorful trout. The McKinnley's felt like they were in heaven. On many an evening they would hold hands, propped up against the strong trunk of the oak, watching the sun set in a soothing array of yellows, reds, and purple haze. When the sun disappeared, stars would slowly come out from hiding, so close it seemed they could almost reach out and touch them. For John and Elizabeth McKinnley, this was the most beautiful place in the world. For their daughter it was quite the opposite.

Gone were the green meadows; replaced by dry, brittle grass. There was no wildlife to speak of, save for an occasional hawk or blue jay that cried out for food, and the river far below was like the shed skin of a snake—only a semblance of its former self. Sarah had been here crying for most of the past two days, and while her tears were now gone, the pain of loss and a great deal of resentment remained.

Elizabeth McKinnley, Sarah's mother, died as a result of infection brought on by a cut from a rusty nail. Not one to watch while work was being done, Elizabeth was helping her husband build his dream—the Bar MC—when her loving hand scraped the lethal nail. The ranch that had claimed the life of Sarah's mother had now taken her father. Sarah had never felt so alone.

Adam LeFloure did his best to comfort Sarah. He was the one to break the horrible news about her father's death, and he had been by her side nearly every moment since. Adam wanted Sarah to sell the Bar MC and he did not hesitate to tell her so. Life, he assured her, would be much better with him back in the East. It did not take much persuading to get Sarah to see things his way. After all, there were too many painful memories on this land for her. The ranch had taken the lives of her parents and interfered with her desire of attending school in the East. Adam didn't have to change Sarah's mind; he only needed to point out what she could already see.

"You can't do that!" Pepper protested, when Sarah told him of her plans.

"This is my ranch now," Sarah said defiantly, "and I'm going to sell it! Then Adam and I are going to get married and leave this God-forsaken valley forever."

"If you sell this ranch to Steele, you'll be going against everything your father stood for. Hell, everything he fought for."

Sarah wasn't moved. "If my father would have sold it, he'd still be alive."

"Then you admit that you think Steele had him killed."

"No, I'm not saying that." Sarah could believe or disbelieve anything if it furthered her cause. "What I am saying is if my father would have sold this place, he probably wouldn't have been on that road."

Pepper had suspected Jason Steele from the moment Adam came riding in with the news, and not for one minute did he believe the sheriff's story of robbers killing McKinnley. No one in town did either, but no one could prove otherwise. The only person who seemed to know for sure was the stranger who brought in McKinnley's body, and he had not been seen since he rode disfigured out of town two days before. Apparently, he was heeding Joe's advice.

"I'm ashamed of you," Pepper said.

"There's nothing I can do to bring my father back," Sarah replied. "And I'm going to do what my father should have done. Sometimes you have to put yourself first."

"That's the trouble with you, Sarah. That's all you've ever done."

Sarah and Pepper did not speak again until the next day on their way into town, and then it wasn't until the false fronts of Canaan Creek were in full view. The bumpy ride in the warm morning air was filled with probing, silent thoughts on both sides of the wagon.

Pepper still had much to say on the subject of selling the ranch to Steele. He also knew he must tread lightly. He did not want to send Sarah deeper inside herself, where any chance of introspection or self-judgement would only be suppressed by stubborn resolve.

By escorting Sarah to the bank, Pepper was in no way agreeing with any part of her decision. He was doing it strictly out of respect for her father, who Pepper reflected on now with a welling of tears.

Pepper Martin and John McKinnley had been friends for over twenty years. They had fought battles together, worked together, and come West together. Neither had saved the other's life, as is common with men who share a special and profound bond. Theirs was a friendship based wholeheartedly on trust, a commodity both men had in abundance and held in high regard.

As far as Pepper was concerned, Sarah's decision to sell the Bar MC to Steele was contemptible, and as they rolled past the Canaan Creek Community Church, he found he could no longer keep silent on the issue.

"If I hadn't been there the day you were born, I would have a hard time believing you were John McKinnley's own flesh and blood."

Sarah was determined not to let the Bar MC be a curse to her like it had to her parents. The ranch was not worth dying for, and no one could convince her otherwise. Sarah would be hard pressed to think of anything worth giving her life for. In her mind, she was simply trying to make the most of a bad situation.

"I don't want to discuss it anymore," she told Pepper. "Nothing you or anyone else can say or do is going to make me change my mind. So, leave it be!"

Down the street, Jason Steele sat proudly in a sun-lit corner of the Onyx. He was enjoying a high priced bottle of brandy, and while it was early to be drinking, Steele was in a celebratory mood. Across the table Sheriff Dan MacLean fidgeted in his seat.

From the day he stepped foot in the valley, Steele vowed to get the Bar MC and now it was moments away from being rightfully his. The Bar MC was to be the cornerstone of the empire Steele wished to establish, and now that he was about to seize it, he could hardly contain himself. For months he had been chipping around the edges, trying to avoid an all out assault on the ranch. Taking the Bar MC by force would have been messy, and could have alerted attention where Steele wanted none. Now all that was to be avoided, and he was actually surprised at how relatively easy the Bar MC was to obtain. He was about to be handed the keys to the kingdom, and he was reveling in the moment. All his plans were coming together.

"Here they come," Joe called from the window, where he was standing watch.

"If I'd a known it was going to be this easy, I would have killed McKinnley long ago," Steele boasted. MacLean smiled nervously at the comment, while Steele refilled his glass. "Take it easy, sheriff, this will all be over in half an hour."

Steele threw back the brandy, then snapped the empty glass down on the table. Ceremoniously he rose to his feet. "Come on, it's time to go buy me a ranch."

The streets of Canaan Creek were quiet. The death of John McKinnley signaled the coming of the end for those remaining in the valley. Over the course of the past three days, the sight of anyone in town other than a Steele man was rare. If there had been any hope for the people in the fight against Steele, it was now buried with John McKinnley. And once word spread about Sarah's decision to sell her father's ranch to Steele, the people presumed the end was upon them. Everyone knew Steele would eventually force them out. The last battle had been fought

9

Keene braved Jason Steele in the bright sunshine of the street. In an instant he had stolen Steele's thunder, and lit a fire under Joe, who was off his post and at the ready, swearing under his breath for letting the man approach as he did.

Standing confidently in front of his roan, Keene showed little effects from his beating three days previous. The swelling was mostly gone bringing back his undoubting eyes. His cuts and bruises were all nearly healed, and even the side of his jaw revealed little trace of Joe's gun-butt.

The man was a sheep among wolves, and his manner seemed to indicate there was no place he'd rather be.

Sarah was noticeably dazed by his charge. She looked over at Steele, whose face now matched the red coat of Keene's roan. "That man's a liar!" Steele bellowed.

"No, it is you who is the liar here," Keene replied coolly. He looked at Sarah. "I watched it happen, Miss McKinnley—I was there. Oh, sure it wasn't Steele who actually killed your father, Joe there did the shooting. But it was all Steele's doing."

Sarah turned to the sheriff. "I thought you said he was killed by robbers."

MacLean rocked back on his heels, stammering, "From what we . . . know so far . . . he was." The sheriff was not convincing, even to himself.

"I can take you to the spot where it happened, Miss McKinnley," Keene said. "And they can hang me from one of the oaks there if we don't find hoofprints that match Steele's stallion and Joe's bay."

Steele looked like a bull trying to hide behind a fence post. "This is outrageous!" he clamored, as if the louder he were, the more likely he was to be believed.

"Is it?" Keene replied. He reached into his shirt pocket and pulled out a .45 casing. "I'll bet you that ranch, Miss McKinnley, that this casing I found next to your father's body matches the bullets in Joe's gun right now."

A long silence followed, all attention now focused on Jason Steele. Steele knew he had been careless with McKinnley's murder, but he never in his wildest imagination thought they were being watched. Steele appeared as guilty as one of the robbers on the cross, and he eyed Joe hoping he would do something about it.

"If you think you're man enough, Preacher Boy, why don't you come over here and check my gun yourself?" Joe taunted him, taking the focus off his boss.

Keene appeared mildly amused. "No—you got me scared."

"Pepper, take me back to the ranch," Sarah said suddenly.

Steele didn't like that. "Hold on a minute! We don't even know who this man is, and you're going to take his word as gospel? What about our deal?"

For Sarah, the man in the street validated what her heart had suspected. Sarah had tried to overlook it, bury it, but this man Keene brought it back out in the open. She didn't know this man, but there was something in his manner, his style, along with his willingness to stand up against Steele, that made Sarah believe him. Why, he even called Jason Steele a liar to his face. Lack of proof no longer seemed a viable excuse for her to sell her father's ranch to the man who may have murdered him. Despite how much she wanted to get rid of the Bar MC, Sarah would not make a deal with her father's killer.

"Not today," Sarah told Steele. "And if you really did kill my father . . . *not ever!*"

Pepper helped Sarah back up onto the buckboard. He had seen only one man handle Jason Steele like this and he had buried him three days before. Stepping to the other side of the wagon, Pepper paused in front of Keene.

"You're welcome to come with us," he offered. "I don't think they'll be throwing a party in your honor anytime soon."

Keene nodded. "I'd be obliged."

Jason Steele burned silently under the awning. His cornerstone was crumbling right before his eyes, and seemingly he could do nothing to stop it. No one had ever called him a liar and lived to tell about it. But Steele didn't do his dirty work, that's what hired gunmen were for, and no one knew that better than Joe Dunbar.

"Hold on!" Joe called out. Keene was putting a boot into the stirrup, about to pull himself up into the saddle. "This ain't finished yet. You don't call Mr. Steele a liar and then ride on outta' here, like it was nothin'. I don't know where you come from, Preacher Boy, but it don't work that way around here."

Joe's face was serious, and his hand flexed near the worn handle of his .45.

"I'm not wearing a gun," Keene said.

"Oh no, not this time, Preacher Boy. You're not getting out of it that easy." Joe gestured to one of his men nearby. "Clay, slap a gunbelt on Preacher Boy, there. Me and him got us some unfinished business to settle."

Clay Donnally loosened his beat-up leather holster and stepped out to the man. With arrogant pleasure, Clay slid the belt around Keene's trim waist, tying it off good and hard.

Keene's eyes never left Joe's.

Sarah rose up in the buckboard. "Sheriff, are you going to let him gun that man down in cold blood?"

"You're not showing much confidence in Joe, ma'am," Keene answered over his shoulder. "But don't worry, I won't kill him."

Joe seethed at the comment. Again, he looked the fool, but more importantly, he was beginning to think about what Keene had said.

The man standing before him showed no fear or reluctance, and his remark, if only for a passing moment, made Joe question himself. Thinking before a battle of any kind is dangerous, especially for a gunman who must react quickly. Thinking allowed hesitation, and Joe knew that could be the difference between living and dying.

The sun was intense and directly behind Joe, making Keene squint to see. The street behind them was empty, with all those watching gathered to the side of the twenty or so feet separating the two men.

Steele watched intently from under the awning of the boardwalk, relieved he was no longer the center of attention.

Sarah, seated again in the buckboard, cupped a hand to her dry lips, while Pepper watched with nostalgic interest, as if he had seen it all before.

"All right, Preacher Boy," Joe finally said. "Are you ready to *die by the sword?*"

Joe's words were still hanging in the tense, hot air when he went for his gun. In the twinkling of an eye, Joe's callused palm was gripping the handle of his Colt .45, while at the same time his index finger slipped easily around the trigger. There was not a wasted movement for he practiced the routine daily. Joe was lightning fast . . . but for the first time, not fast enough.

Keene slid out the borrowed .45 and had it leveled before Joe could clear leather.

Joe stood frozen, his .45 half-out of the holster. True to his word, the man facing him did not shoot.

Keene kept the steel barrel of the six-shooter steady and even. "Can I leave now?" he asked.

10

No one spoke on the way back to the ranch. Pepper and Sarah were both silently evaluating what had just transpired in the street in front of the bank, along with its coming impact. The outcome of Keene's confrontation with Joe was by no means an ending. If anything it was a new beginning, with fresh players now involved in an old and deadly game.

Pepper knew Steele would not let the situation lie. Having the Bar MC snatched from his covetous hands, especially when it was so close to being his, would only serve to strengthen Steele's intent. Steele could not be put off—impeded perhaps, but never put off. Men like Steele did not become feared and powerful by withdrawing from their pursuits. They expected obstacles, sometimes even courted them for the challenge. For Pepper, it was not a matter of would Steele strike at them again; but rather *when* would he strike, and more importantly . . . how?

The man they knew only as Keene trailed peaceably behind, keeping to the side of the cloud of dust kicked up by the rolling wheels of the buckboard. His calm demeanor gave no indication of the volatile situation he left behind. Roan and rider were one, and at ease.

Several times Sarah turned in her seat to peer at the man. Once she caught herself staring intently at him, completely lost in his presence. It wasn't until Keene smiled warmly back at her that Sarah spun back around, embarrassed.

There was something both familiar and comforting about this man, Sarah thought. Watching him out in the street battling Joe gave Sarah a curious inner excitement. A kind she had never felt before. Who was this man? And why had he risked his life to tell her the truth about her father's death? What did he have to gain from that? There must be something. After all, Sarah could not imagine doing anything if it didn't serve her interest in some way.

Arriving back at the Bar MC, Pepper and Keene broke down the wagon and tended to the horses while Sarah went inside to prepare breakfast.

Pepper watched Keene casually, taking note of how carefully he cared for his roan. Keene watered the horse, hand fed it barley and some carrots he pulled out of his saddlebag, and rubbed it down before he finally dipped a hand in the trough to have a drink. Pepper knew that how a man treated his mount went a long way on how he might treat a man.

They talked as they worked, Pepper purposely avoiding any discussion about what had occurred in town. Instead,

Pepper made small talk and answered Keene's general queries about the ranch and the valley.

He knew the man was a stranger to the Kern River Valley, but he got a sense that Keene knew all the answers to his questions before he asked, and was probably better informed than he was letting on.

When they finished, Pepper and Keene went inside where the aroma of baking biscuits, frying bacon, and fresh coffee all fought for equal billing. Pepper loved the smell of breakfast. It reminded him of his life as a boy back on his folks' Texas farm.

Seated around the oak table they ate slowly, still avoiding the topic of what happened earlier that morning. Casually, Sarah glimpsed Keene eat. She was amazed at how refined he seemed to be—Keene used his napkin to wipe the corners of his mouth after nearly every bite. His every action, even at the table, seemed smooth and effortless. She had so many questions for this man, and while she wanted to blurt them all out at once, Sarah wasn't sure she was ready for the answers. She was cleaning away the empty breakfast plates when she finally found the courage to ask.

"Did he suffer . . . my father . . . after they shot him?"

"No, it happened very fast," Keene answered, lifting his coffee cup. "He probably didn't feel a thing."

A tear began to form in Sarah's eye. "What happened? Why did they shoot him?"

"They had the road to the bridge blocked," Keene explained. "Steele tried to get your father to sell the ranch to him, and when he refused, Steele attempted to blackmail him. That's when your father tried to ride herd through them, and Joe shot him."

"Back up there a minute," Pepper chimed in. "How was Steele planning to blackmail him?"

Keene looked at Sarah over the top of his coffee cup. "Steele mentioned something about some trouble you got into a few months back in Mojave."

His answer made Sarah anxious. Pepper reacted, as well.

"Your father had a great deal of money on him," Keene commented.

Sarah knew her father had gone to the bank the morning of his death, but she was unaware that he had closed out their account. In all the confusion and activity of the past few days, Sarah had simply forgotten to check on the status of her father's financial affairs. And with the money she was going to receive from selling the ranch to Steele, the bank account was not a priority.

She looked directly at Pepper. "Do you know why my father was carrying so much money?"

Pepper hesitated. "He closed out his account at the bank."

"Why?"

"So he could send you to school."

The answer slammed into Sarah. The argument with her father the night before his death leaped into her mind, and guilt rushed in with it.

Sarah needed a moment to collect her thoughts. Finally she asked, "Why didn't you tell me this before?"

"I thought it best if a little time passed," Pepper said. "I didn't want you blaming yourself for what happened."

"You had no right to do that, Pepper Martin!"

"I know," Pepper agreed, "and I'm sorry. But I knew things were gonna be hard enough on you as it was."

Sarah stepped over to her father's chair, clutching the high leather back for support. She closed her eyes hoping this was all just a bad dream. Maybe when she opened her eyes again, she would be back in her bed, a young girl, looking up at the arched pine ceiling in her room. Her world would be set right, and if she listened carefully, she might even be able to hear the cheerful voice of her mother downstairs.

But it wasn't a dream. She opened her eyes, fighting back tears. "Part of me wanted to sell this place out of resentment towards my father," Sarah said. "I honestly felt he cared more for this ranch than he did for me."

"That's not true," Pepper replied, "not by a long shot. Your father cared about you more than anything in this world. You have to understand the fix he was in. When this drought started two years ago, we had close to thirty hands on the payroll. Now, not one of them is left.

"John tried to keep 'em working for as long as he could, but eventually, one-by-one, he had to let 'em go. Your father couldn't bring himself to make a man go hungry so he could send his daughter to school."

Sarah had been wrapped up in her own affairs giving little thought to her father's situation. She knew in her heart that she wasn't responsible for his death, but that didn't ease the guilt that now consumed her. It was, after all, her selfishness that put her father on that road with Steele and his men.

When she looked up from the chair, she realized Keene was gone. At some point he had slipped out unnoticed, leaving them to their family business.

Moments later when the front door flew open, Sarah felt relieved that Keene had returned. She was disappointed to find it was Adam LeFloure.

"Sarah, my dear, what happened?" he said, rushing to her side. "They told me in town you changed your mind about selling this insufferable ranch."

"I have," Sarah answered.

"Why? What about our plans to leave and get married?"

"I need some time, Adam. I can't think about that right now."

It was true; Sarah did have a great deal on her mind. And the one thought she found herself coming back to was Keene.

Three days after the episode on the street, Steele sat his stallion on a ridge also contemplating the man. Keene had embarrassed him and would be made to pay.

But first, Steele would need to find out Keene's background. Where did he come from? And why was he here in the Kern River Valley? Was it by chance, or had McKinnley hired Keene to go up against Steele? Steele decided to do some checking. Not many men could beat Joe to the draw, so this man must have some sort of reputation . . . somewhere.

Steele looked out across the vast wasteland that was his kingdom. The dry grass was littered with dead cattle and sheep, their reeking carcasses bloated and pointing skyward. The sun and the drought were killing the valley one cow, one sheep at a time.

"What are we gonna do if Sarah McKinnley doesn't sell?" Joe asked. "If we don't get water soon, there won't be no cattle left."

"Joe, I'm disappointed in you," Steele said. He was gazing off into the hills, as if focused on some distant dream. "You have no vision. Acquiring the Bar MC is not just about water, it's about the future. When I get McKinnley's ranch, and make no mistake about it, I will get it—I'll own this whole valley. Land is power, Joe. And powerful people become great things, like governors and presidents."

Steele was correct; Joe had no vision. A gunfighter's life was not planned so much as it was prolonged.

Joe pushed his hat back on his head. "How you figure on changin' Sarah McKinnley's mind?"

"By using the greatest motivator in the world, Joe . . . *Fear.*"

11

Sarah scooped up the brown eggs and placed them in the basket she cradled in her left arm. She moved busily through the hen house nest to nest, Adam hovering close at her side. He was beginning to annoy her.

She hated that Adam chose each step delicately, trying his best not to scuff or dirty the shine on his New York bought boots. And when he lifted his monogrammed handkerchief to his nose to keep from smelling the foul hen house air, Sarah decided she'd had enough. Besides, she was tired of the conversation.

"Adam, I don't want to talk about this anymore."

"He might be an outlaw," Adam warned, "you don't know."

"Because he's fast with a gun? Don't be silly." Sarah added another egg to her basket. "Just because he's one, doesn't mean he's the other. Look at you—you're a man, but you're walking around in here like an old woman. Besides, don't most outlaws wear a gun?" Sarah ducked her head out the hen house door and started across the yard.

"We can't be too careful," Adam cautioned, chasing after her.

On the porch, Sarah paused to observe the alleged gunman of whom Adam spoke. Keene was headed for the barn carrying a shovel, his muscular arms glistening with hard-work sweat. He was helping Pepper mend a portion of the corral, and they had been at it most of the morning.

The sound of approaching horses directed Sarah's attention out to the front gate of the ranch. Cantering in under the Bar MC sign was Jason Steele and Joe Dunbar.

Pepper saw them, also, and grabbed up McKinnley's Winchester Sarah had given him as a keepsake. He joined Sarah on the front porch as the two rode up.

"Hello again, Miss McKinnley," Steele greeted in his own condescending way. He raised up to throw a leg over the saddle.

"No need to get down," Sarah told him. "You won't be staying that long."

The comment chafed the smile off of Steele's face. "Well now, I thought a man was innocent until proven guilty," he stated, settling back down in the saddle.

"With one of your men as sheriff?" Pepper spoke up. "Justice ain't exactly being served that way, is it? But then, isn't that the way you planned it?"

Steele rested a gloved hand on his pommel, grinning. "Surely, you didn't believe all those lies that man was spouting?" He raised up in the stirrups. "Where is the man everyone is talking about?"

Just then, a hand gave a firm slap to the rump of Steele's mount. The stallion jerked out sideways, startled. "This a private conversation," Keene said, "or can anybody join in?" He stepped nonchalantly between Joe and Steele, up onto the porch.

At the site of Keene, Joe stiffened in his saddle, while Steele fought his agitated horse back under control. Behind his politician's smile, Steele was clearly annoyed.

"There's the man of the hour," Steele said. "That was quite a show you put on the other day."

Keene didn't reply, instead he gave Joe a disinterested look.

Joe's face was taut. The mere mention of the encounter with Keene embarrassed Joe, and that made him mad. Joe tried to hide his shame by staring the man down, but Keene simply ignored him.

"If you rode all the way out here to talk about the ranch, you're wasting your time," Sarah told Steele. "And mine."

"Shouldn't we at least hear what he has to say?" Adam spoke up.

Sarah's blue eyes burned out at Steele. "Adam, I am not going to sell my father's ranch to the man that murdered him."

"Miss McKinnley, I understand you had some trouble a few months back in Mojave," Steele stated roughly. "I hear the sheriff there would be very interested to know where you are." Steele's caustic grin was back and he could sense Sarah growing unnerved at the mere subject of Mojave. "Now if you'd reconsider selling the Bar MC to me, a ranch I understand you really don't want anyway, I would be of no mind to tell the sheriff of Mojave where he could find you."

The basket of eggs under Sarah's arm began to quiver. Steele had found a crack in her tough exterior.

Pepper raised up his Winchester. "Conversation's over! Now, you two, get out of here!"

Joe scowled. He didn't like a rifle being aimed in his direction. "I wouldn't point that thing unless I was man enough to use it," he warned.

Pepper cocked the rifle. "My thought exactly."

Steele yanked the stallion around in a quarter-turn. "You think about it, Miss McKinnley. Prison's a tough place for a woman—if you even get that far."

The last comment managed to work its way deep into Sarah's fears. And when Steele followed it with a wicked laugh, Sarah gasped, dropping the basket of eggs on the wood planking of the porch. Her fearful eyes were locked on Steele who was now wearing the Devil's grin. He held her transfixed, his dark, cunning eyes boring into her, cutting a path all the way down to Sarah's fragile soul.

At that moment Sarah became afraid of Steele. She turned quickly and ran into the house, sobbing.

Keene stepped forward. "It isn't going to work, Steele. You've already tried to play that hand."

Steele laughed again. He was feeling good about himself now that he was back dealing the cards. "This is a new game, mister—a whole new game!" He jerked the stallion around and started off.

"You and me, we're not done yet, Preacher Boy," Joe added. He galloped off to join Steele. Both men laughed loudly as they left the front gate of the Bar MC.

Sarah sat in her father's chair, trembling. She held a hand to her mouth, while Adam attempted to calm her by resting a reassuring hand on her back. She didn't like it there.

"Sarah, I beg of you," Adam pleaded. "Sell this horrible place to Steele and let's get out of here. It's not worth all this."

Pepper, back inside, didn't appreciate the advice. He was becoming tired of Adam's constant prodding.

"How did he find out about Mojave?" Sarah sniffled, wiping a hand at her tears.

"Sarah?" It was Keene and his voice soothed her. "If you don't mind me asking, what exactly did happen in Mojave?"

Adam LeFloure tore himself off the arm of the chair. "We do mind your asking, mister! This is none of your business!"

"Adam!" Sarah called, surprised by his sudden and unprovoked hostility towards Keene. It was a side of Adam she had never seen.

"It's alright," Keene said. "I understand if you don't want to tell me. Adam is right, it's none of my business."

"No—I'll tell you." Sarah found the words came out on their own.

"Why?" Adam objected.

"Because . . . I think he should know."

Pepper watched Adam sulk off into the corner. He didn't understand Adam's animosity towards Keene. Was it jealousy or something more to it than that?

Sarah took a slow, deep breath. She had thought the incident in Mojave was behind her. "A few months ago, I got mad at my father because he wouldn't send me to school back East," she began. "We'd had the same argument a number of times, so I decided that if he wouldn't send me, I was going to get on the stage and go there myself. I know now it was foolish, but I was very angry at the time."

Keene smiled. "You do this kind of thing often?"

"Keep listening," Pepper chuckled, "it gets better."

A sheepish smile broke out across Sarah's red face. Adam was the only one in the room who did not feel better.

"As I was saying," Sarah continued, "the stage I was on stopped for the night in Mojave. It's a railroad town and it's pretty wild there, and that also goes for the law. Late that evening, the sheriff busted into my hotel room and tried to . . . he broke in and I shot him."

"You always carry a gun?" Keene asked.

"It was an old derringer that belonged to my father. I brought it along just in case. Good thing, too."

"Did you kill him?"

"No, but I messed up his face pretty bad. The desk clerk hid me and got me out of town before the sheriff and his deputies could find me."

"Then you didn't break the law," Keene said.

"We'd heard," Pepper commented, "that the sheriff there may have been run out of town, or even killed, but we couldn't confirm it. John sent a telegram checking into it, but he hadn't heard anything back."

Sarah was again troubled. "If that sheriff finds me, he'll kill me. He was screaming that after I shot him."

"Don't worry," Keene assured her. "Steele's probably bluffing, anyhow. But even if he isn't it, we won't let anybody take you."

Adam didn't like the way Keene said that, although it did make Sarah feel better.

The next day Sarah awoke early. She dressed in her finest riding pants, white blouse, and a western hat she had never worn that her father bought her in Denver. It was a calm, cool morning, and the dawning gray sky still held a handful of stars as Sarah left the front gate of the Bar MC atop her father's appaloosa. She planned to spend the day thinking and getting reacquainted with the ranch she had inherited. Perhaps a look around with a new perspective would shed some light and give her some guidance for the situation now facing her.

Sarah had been forced to grow up a lot during the past week. What normally would have taken years to learn and hone had been thrust upon Sarah in only a few days. She felt older.

She now owned the ranch she wanted her father to sell only days before. Keeping the Bar MC was not in her plans, and she was not, for obvious reasons, going to sell it to Jason Steele.

Ironically, Sarah now found herself facing the same dilemma as her father: how to keep Jason Steele from taking the Bar MC?

Sarah's motives were certainly different from her father's, but they were now united in purpose. And while John McKinnley had been willing to go to his grave to keep the ranch away from Steele, Sarah did not feel so strongly. She was not willing to die for the Bar MC, and the thought of possibly going to prison, as Steele put it, made her less inclined to put up a fight.

All morning Sarah explored the dry, brittle pines for a solution, hoping they would speak to her through their knowing silence. When the afternoon came, she found herself examining the sun-baked meadows as if her answers lay somewhere hidden in the brown grass. But the land was quiet and still, giving up no hidden secrets, and offering up only a deafening silence that added to Sarah's loneliness.

If anything came of this, it was that Sarah now had a new understanding of her father, and a newfound respect. She remembered him saying, *Doing the right thing isn't always the easiest road to travel, but it's always the right road.* Sarah didn't know if she could travel that road.

The day burned on and Sarah led the appaloosa back towards the ranch. The more answers she tried to come up with, the more problems seemed to present themselves. She was no closer to a solution now than when she had left the ranch that morning. Maybe, she considered at one point, there was no solution.

She did disagree with her father on one fundamental point: principles seemed a poor thing to die for. And if Steele's threat to bring in the sheriff of Mojave was just that, a threat, he could still try and take the Bar MC by force. Sarah had told her father he wouldn't stand a chance if Steele decided to do that, why would she? The more she thought about it, the more troubled she became.

Hot, thirsty, and discouraged, Sarah led the appaloosa to the Kern River bed. A narrow path of water trickled down its center, bending around a large boulder before it disappeared. She found herself in a secluded bower, a good place to get out of the sun and drink some water before heading back home.

She dismounted and the appaloosa dropped its head, sniffing at the clear water before it drank. She removed her hat and knelt beside. The cold water looked inviting and felt refreshing when she splashed it across her face. Cupping the water in her hands, Sarah drank slow and deep. There wasn't much water—she could step across it— but what little there was tasted good.

Slowly, Sarah found herself relaxing. She would have liked to stay longer, but she wanted to make a pass by the dam before heading back. She knew Pepper would worry if she wasn't home before dark.

Just five more minutes . . .

Unexpectedly, the appaloosa's head shot up. It was then that Sarah heard the heart-stopping cry of the wild beast above her.

12

The fierce cry of the mountain lion overpowered Sarah. She was leaning down to drink, and heard its forbidding call before she could actually see the wild cat. Fear took hold of her body. Her legs went numb beneath her and Sarah lost her balance, falling back on her hands into the tiny stream. Less than ten feet separated her from the snarling cat perched on the edge of a flat rock above her.

Sarah pulled her knees up close to her chest and coughed from lack of breath. She was scared like she'd never been scared before, and adding to her fear was the knowledge that the chances of anyone finding her was remote, since Sarah herself wasn't sure where she was going when she rode off that morning.

She reached up from the ground and grabbed hold of the appaloosa's reins. The frightened horse moved about restlessly, keeping the mountain lion on the rock above.

Sarah knew she must keep hold of the reins. With the big horse there, the cat would stay away.

The mountain lion was large—close to five-feet from nose to tail—with shrunken sides, exposing its bony rib cage underneath. Food for the cat had been scarce since most of the other valley creatures were moving higher and higher into the Sierra in their own quest for food and water. The hungry lion displayed its sharp-curved fangs, pacing anxiously above its prisoner.

Below, the appaloosa continued to blow and stomp, and Sarah had to fight hard to keep the horse from running off. She decided she must get to her feet. Then she could try to climb into the saddle and ride the appaloosa to safety.

She pushed up from her knees, hoping there would be life in her wobbly legs. It took a moment, but her legs caught, struggling to hold the weight of her body. She was almost standing when the fearful horse reared up. Sarah was nearly kicked in the head, and she rolled out of the way just in time. The quick move saved her, but it forced her to loosen her grip on the reins. The scared appaloosa sprinted off, disappearing down the riverbed.

Sarah screamed!

The cat answered with a violent and terrifying cry.

Screaming was all Sarah could think to do, and between screams she began to make all the promises one makes to their God when faced with a life or death situation. No longer would Sarah doubt her father's faith; no longer would Sarah be so selfish; no longer . . . the list grew and grew. If Sarah were delivered safely from this mountain lion, she would become the kindest, most humble individual the Kern River Valley would ever know.

"Sarah? . . . Sarah?" The voice belonged to Keene.

"Over here!" Sarah called in relief. "Hurry!"

Keene emerged from around the boulder mound atop the roan, and the big cat greeted him with a deafening roar in warning.

"Shoot him!" Sarah shouted.

"I can't. I don't carry a gun, remember."

"Oh, that's just great!"

The cat's sides pulsed with rage at Keene's presence. Its pace quickened and its cries became more intense.

Keene dismounted carefully, studying the situation. The ears of his roan were pricked at attention, and occasionally the horse would blow as if telling the lion he was not afraid.

Using guarded, efficient steps, Keene slowly made his way toward Sarah, cautiously maneuvering himself between her and the mountain lion.

Sarah beheld Keene in wonder. He moved daringly, his face intense without fear. She recalled Adam the day before in the hen house. This man before her was everything Adam was not. Could Keene really be an outlaw, as Adam proposed? Sarah didn't think so, but how was he able to handle himself so assuredly in every situation, and with so much confidence? Even at this moment, with no gun for protection, he faced a vicious mountain lion with no disposition of fear or resistance. It was as if he had done it a hundred times before.

Having positioned himself between the mountain lion and Sarah, Keene became completely still. Once, Sarah began to speak but he threw a hand up behind him, and she knew to stop. It reminded her of the first day she watched Keene out in the street with Joe. The same focussed, confident stare, which had looked out at Joe, was now locked on the dangerous mountain lion above.

The hungry cat roared its disapproval. It didn't like being stared down, but with each intense moment, its cries became less challenging.

To Sarah's amazement, Keene appeared to somehow be communicating with the animal, as if the cat were another gunman and Keene were telling it to pack its gun and go quietly. Sarah would never have believed it if she weren't there to witness it herself. Before her very eyes, Keene was reducing the once threatening mountain lion to a harmless alley cat.

Keene held firm, while the wild cat moved about uneasily, every once in a while letting out a loud cry in an attempt to save face. Astounded, Sarah watched the game being played out for several minutes.

Abruptly, Keene stepped forward, waving his hands in the air and yelling, "Get out of here!" and the mountain lion obeyed, turning tail, disappearing into the brush above.

Keene turned quickly on his heels. "You okay?"

Sarah slumped down in relief. "Who are you?"

He only smiled. After several moments, Keene helped Sarah to her feet. They were shaky at first, but she could stand.

"How did you find me?" she asked.

"Pepper didn't like the idea of you riding off alone. He said if I didn't find you at your father's grave, I might want to check near the dam." Keene pointed. "Isn't it up that way? I'd like to see it."

Pine trees threw their reflections out across the still water of the man-made reservoir, and tired cattle rested underneath the branches that filtered out the late afternoon sun. Sarah found a rock in some shade and sat down.

The man she knew only as Keene sat next to her, his eyes inspecting the man-made lake thoughtfully. Sarah couldn't let it go: who was this man? He had a presence beyond words that she found very appealing.

"It's interesting," Keene finally spoke up, "that such a calm and peaceful place could be the focus of so much fighting and death." A trace of sadness moved across Sarah's face. "What's wrong?" he asked.

"A few days ago, I wanted to sell this ranch to get back at my father because I thought he cared more for it than he did for me. And now that I don't want to sell, I have to."

"Sarah, don't let Steele blackmail you into selling this ranch."

"I don't have a choice. What if he's serious about bringing that sheriff here?"

"For all we know he's bluffing," Keene replied. "We'll check into it, but you've got to hold out, at least for a little while."

Sarah was still scared. "If I sell it, I get something for it. If I don't, Steele will just take it from us. How would we stop him?"

"Sarah, I promise you, Steele will not get this ranch. Trust me."

"Trust you?" Sarah laughed. "I don't even know you." She got up and started to say something else, but stopped. "You know, the funny thing is, I do trust you." She felt odd saying it, but she felt it in her heart.

Returning to the riverbed, Sarah was relieved to find no sign of the mountain lion, and the appaloosa was back drinking next to the roan. The roan appeared to have the same calming effect on the appaloosa that Keene had on Sarah.

"You know, you never did answer me," Sarah said. "Who are you?"

Keene gave the roan an affectionate rub underneath its neck. "Is it really that important?"

"I think it is," Sarah said honestly. "Don't I have a right to know who I'm putting my trust in?"

"Tell you what. I'll answer that, if you tell me why you're planning to marry a man you're not in love with."

"How do you know I'm not in love with him?"

"It wasn't hard to figure out. It's the way you look at him. There's no spark."

His comment put Sarah on the defense, as the truth often did. "You're something else," she said. "Fast with a gun, you can talk to a mountain lion, and if that wasn't enough, you know just what people are feeling."

"Alright, tell me I'm wrong."

Sarah couldn't, and she knew it. She searched desperately for a response, but the truth left her speechless. She was about to offer up a rebuttal when the cock of a pistol brought her up short.

Two men were behind them. The closest, a tall, dark-skinned man pointed a six-gun. "Well now, I'll just bet you're Sarah McKinnley," he said. "And you must be the stranger everyone's talkin' about."

"Don't look like much to me, Reiger." It was the bearded man with him. His three separated teeth, in an otherwise empty tobacco-stained mouth, earned him the nickname, Ivory.

"You know who we are," Keene said evenly, "now, who are you?"

Ivory stepped up. "Who we are ain't important, mister. We come from Mojave for the girl." He let out a nasty spit of tobacco near Keene's boot. "Sheriff there wants to have a few words with her."

"I don't see any badges," Keene said.

"Mister, I'm pointin' my badge!" Reiger replied shortly.

Ivory's look turned fierce. He noticed Keene's attention going beyond them, and at one point Ivory even turned to check behind him, but nothing was there. It disturbed him.

It bothered Reiger, as well. "What are you thinkin' about, mister? I know it ain't your choices, cause you ain't got none."

"Let's get this over with," Ivory told Reiger. "Shoot him and we'll take the girl."

Sarah gasped. She slid up behind Keene for protection, clutching his arms tightly.

"Before I did that I would take a peek behind you," Keene cautioned. "That gun blast is liable to bring that big cat right down on top of you."

Reiger and Ivory both laughed—the nerve of this man.

"I don't know about you," Keene went on, "but I think I'd rather take my chances getting shot than mauled by a hungry mountain lion."

Both men wanted to look, but to turn would be to buy into what the man was saying. Ivory attempted to laugh it off. "I heard about you, mister. They say you tried to talk your way out of the beatin' you got from Joe Dunbar. Well, it ain't gonna work this time, neither." Ivory turned to Reiger. "Shoot him!"

The mountain lion *roared* behind them.

Reiger wheeled to shoot at the cat and that's when Keene jumped forward. He knocked the pistol out of the bigger man's hand, then put him down with a heavy fist to the jaw.

Ivory, distracted for a brief second by the mountain lion, went for his gun. Keene kicked out with his leg and caught the older man in the stomach. When he buckled, Keene snatched the .45 Ivory had drawn, then pushed him to the ground. Keene kept the pistol on the two men as the mountain lion cried out from above.

"Sarah, get on your horse," Keene said over his shoulder.

Ivory gagged from the tobacco he had swallowed when he was kicked, while Reiger rubbed his jaw. It was painful and beginning to swell.

Keene backed up and swung into the saddle. "You boys be careful now, because that mountain lion there is powerful hungry. He wanted a piece of me earlier."

"You can't leave us here with that thing," Reiger pleaded.

"Why not?" Keene replied. "You were going to leave me here with a bullet in my head."

"If you was decent at all, you'd leave us one of our guns," Ivory said.

"I'll make you a deal. Tell me who sent you and I'll throw one down."

"Don't do that!" Sarah protested.

Ivory couldn't wait to speak up, and when Reiger tried to stop him, Ivory slapped him down. "Jason Steele," Ivory confessed. "He wanted us to bring him the girl so he could force her to sign over her ranch. There, I told you, now give us that gun."

Keene began unloading the chamber of Reiger's six-shooter.

"Oh, that's real funny, mister," Reiger sneered. He slapped Ivory. "See, I told you not to tell him."

"Shut up!" Ivory replied angrily.

The big cat paced and roared from above.

Keene smiled. "If you can catch him, I hear mountain lion tastes real good."

Sarah didn't have much to say on the way back to the ranch. She found it difficult to put all the thoughts swirling in her head into words. They were nearly home when she suddenly turned in the saddle and said, "Who are you?"

13

Dusk settled over the Kern River Valley. The red sun slipped slowly from view and almost imperceptibly the night sky assumed a palette of fading blue and pink. One by one twinkling stars appeared, and a cool breeze pushed away the lingering afternoon heat. Two days had passed since Sarah's encounter with the mountain lion, and from the moment she had returned to the ranch, she had not stopped talking about the man she knew only as Keene.

"You should've seen him," Sarah raved to Pepper. "It was like he could actually talk to the mountain lion. And when Steele's men showed up, it was like he brought it back. I never saw anything like it."

From his seat on the porch rail Pepper watched the sparks dancing in her eyes. This was the most excited he had ever seen Sarah.

Like her father, Pepper was more than a little suspicious of Adam. He especially didn't care for the way Adam was attempting to get Sarah to sell the ranch to Steele. He was pleased to see Sarah taking a liking to someone other than Adam, but was she falling in love with Keene? Pepper didn't know, and he knew better than to ask.

Sarah couldn't get Keene out of her thoughts, nor did she want to. "Why doesn't he stay with us at night? Where does he go?"

"I don't know," Pepper answered, starting the makings of a cigarette. "Sometimes a man gets used to sleepin' under the stars, he finds he can't put his head down anyplace else."

"How could anyone not sleep better with a roof over their head?"

Pepper lit his smoke, taking in the clear night sky. Sarah, meanwhile, thought more about his answer. There was an air of isolation about Keene accentuated by his leaving the ranch every night. He was their friend and ally, but at the same time, both she and Pepper felt far removed from him.

"Do you think he's an outlaw?" Sarah finally asked.

The thought had crossed Pepper's mind. Most men who were as fast to the draw as Keene usually carried some kind of past with them, but there was something in this man's genteel, civilized manner that seemed to rule out the possibility. The fact that he didn't wear a gun told Pepper that if Keene did have something disreputable in his past, he was attempting to leave it there.

"I don't know," Pepper answered. "I don't believe so. And if he is or was, it seems he's tryin' to make good on it now. Whatever his story, I'm damn glad he's on our side."

Regrettably though, Pepper didn't believe that Keene alone would be enough to make the difference between saving or losing the ranch. True, this man had performed some amazing deeds and, thus far, held Steele in check, but the reality of the situation was plain to see. Pepper knew if Steele decided to take the Bar MC by force it would be a simple problem of mathematics: Steele would outnumber them nearly ten-to-one.

And why hadn't Steele attempted a run at the ranch? Steele was a cold-blooded killer, but Pepper also knew Steele was a politician first. If he could seize the ranch covertly, fewer people in high places were likely to find out. Steele didn't care if he was surrounded by an air of impropriety—what politician wasn't? He just wanted to make sure the bodies, quite literally in this case, remained buried. Pepper had come across men like Jason Steele before. They believed the ends justified the means, and their goal was always to make sure that the means appeared as appealing and palatable as possible, even if they had to hold their nose to taste its fruits.

So far, Steele had attempted blackmail, kidnapping, and even murder to get the Bar MC. His failure only served to increase his appetite for the ranch.

The next morning a vanilla sky greeted the rising sun. Streaks of gray clouds drifted far off along the eastern peaks, and the afternoon wind still lay sleeping in the branches of the surrounding pines.

Keene rode into the Bar MC looking fresh and alert. Pepper, pleased to have Keene around, came outside to greet him.

"Just in time for breakfast," he told him. "I'll tell you what, fast with a gun and good timin' to boot. You better be careful, I know a lot of women who'd consider those irresistible qualities."

Keene grinned. "What do you say we try and keep that a secret?" He followed Pepper inside the house.

"Sarah will be down in a minute," Pepper informed him. "She's getting herself all gussied up."

"Oh, I am not, Pepper Martin," Sarah scolded, bursting into the kitchen. Her eyes were bright and happy, like a kid in a candy store. "I only want to look presentable."

Pepper grabbed a plate of eggs off the stove and slid them onto the table. "I hope you can eat your eggs without biscuits," Pepper said. "We're all out of flour."

"Getting low on supplies?" Keene asked.

Pepper nodded. "We could use a few things."

"I feel like a prisoner on this ranch," Sarah complained. They had not been in Canaan Creek since the incident in front of the bank, and with Steele's latest attempt to grab Sarah, both Pepper and Keene thought it safer for them to remain close to the ranch.

"Maybe its time to make a run into town," Keene suggested.

"Isn't that kind of risky?" Sarah said.

"We'll have to do it sometime," Keene replied. "Might as well be now."

Pepper picked up the coffeepot. "What about Sarah? Steele already tried to grab her once."

"I'm going with you!"

"That's probably not a good idea," Keene said.

"And why not? They're not going to shoot a woman, now are they?"

"I wouldn't put anything past Steele at this point," Pepper said, pouring a cup of coffee.

"Well, I'm going anyway." Sarah insisted. She smiled over at Keene. "Besides, nothing is going to happen to me if you're there."

"Let's be smart about this," Keene said. "The more targets we give Steele, the more shots he's going to take. I'll go into town."

Sarah felt her heart jump. "Alone?"

"We can't ask you to do that," Pepper said. "This isn't your fight."

"You didn't ask, I volunteered. And you forget, this became my fight the minute I called Jason Steele a liar out there on the street. As long as I'm here, we're in this together."

His comment brought up an issue burning in Sarah's mind. "And why are you still here? You could ride out of this at anytime. What reason do you have for risking your life for us?"

Pepper had wrestled with it, as well. He was curious what Keene's answer might be.

"I saw a man murdered—I can't walk away from that."

"You didn't walk away," Sarah replied. "You brought my father in and told everyone who murdered him. What else is left for you to do? Getting yourself killed is not going to bring my father back."

"Maybe I want to see Steele pay for what he did."

Sarah wasn't convinced. "Well, that's very noble of you, but why? Nobody risks their life for nothing. There must be something you stand to gain, but maybe you don't want us to know what that is."

"*What does it profit a man to gain the whole world, but lose his soul?*" Keene replied.

Sarah laughed. "Listen to you drawing out Bible verses like you were drawing a gun. I heard about you preaching to Joe in the Onyx. My father believed all that crazy stuff, too, and look where it got him . . . he's dead."

"*If a man keeps my saying, he will never see death.*"

Sarah didn't have a reply for that.

Keene pulled back gently on the traces and the buckboard team came to a stop outside the Kern River Valley Mercantile & Exchange. A stiff wind was kicking up out of the north, stirring up the red dirt and rattling the storefront signs. Keene had convinced them to let him go to town alone, and while Sarah and Pepper for differing reasons did not like it, they were both grateful.

Eli Billings—owner/proprietor of the KRVM&E—was reading a newspaper spread out over the counter top when Keene entered. A blast of wind came with him, rustling the paper from underneath Eli's black elbows.

The "Merc," as it was known, was cozy rather than small. A general store in every sense of the word, a person going to the Merc could just as easily leave with an assortment of canned goods and dry foods as he could a saddle, a fly, or a picket pin, and what wasn't in stock could quickly be ordered.

Eli recognized Keene right off, and he watched quietly as Keene made his way, in no particular order, around the store. Eli needed a moment to summon up the courage to approach Keene, not out of fear, but respect.

"You know, you sure put on some show here the other day," Eli said, moving out from behind the counter. He made his long fingers into a pistol. "Whippin' that ol' gun out on Joe like you done." He then dropped his voice down deep. "*Can I leave now?*" he imitated Keene. Eli cackled, "Yes sir, you made a lot of folks proud around here that day, I can tell you that." He thrust out his hand. "Eli Billings is my name and if only half the stuff I've heard about you is true, you've the makin's of a legend."

"And what is it that you've heard?" Keene said, shaking his hand.

"Well, most think you's a gunman from New Mexico way. Others think you may be a retired lawman from Texas. Some have even said a preacher with a fast draw."

"What do you say?"

Eli smiled. "I say you's anybody you want to be. Finally someone's put Steele and his cutthroats in their place."

Keene continued his shopping, selecting a wide range of supplies. Each time his arms would fill up he would bring the items over to the counter where Eli would mark them down on a piece of paper with a pencil he took from behind his ear. When he finished, Keene pointed to the cartridges that were neatly stacked behind the counter. "Let's add to that list about five hundred rounds of those."

Eli's drooping, blood-shot eyes met Keene's—he knew what the bullets were for. Like everyone else in the valley, Eli figured Steele would eventually make his run on the Bar MC. Eli slipped out from behind the counter and popped off the lid of an empty pickle barrel. "Probably cause less of a fuss to carry all those in here, wouldn't you think?"

Keene slid over the counter and began handing the boxes of cartridges to Eli who placed them in the barrel. When they finished, Keene asked what he owed.

"Let's see," Eli began, his old bones creaking as he straightened up. He grabbed up the piece of paper off the counter and began a running inventory. There were canned beans, flour, coffee, chipped beef, cider, tobacco, cornmeal, tea, and he said with a wink, "let's not forget a barrel of pickles."

They were stacking the supplies in crates when the front door pushed open and a gust of wind came rushing in. It was Preacher Jed Boyd stepping inside.

"Hey there, Preach," Eli greeted.

"I don't know what it was, but I was sitting over in the church just now going over Sunday's sermon when I suddenly had the strangest urge to come to your store." Boyd looked over at Keene. "Now, I think I know why."

Boyd helped Keene and Eli carry the supplies out to the wagon. The wind was getting stronger, and red dust whipped up into their eyes. Keene set the pickle barrel down next to the wagon. "Go ahead and put those crates in the bed," he instructed. He reached behind the seat and pulled out a tarp and some rope. Boyd was watching his every move.

"Something on your mind, Preacher?" Keene asked.

"I don't know what it is," Boyd answered, "but I have this strange feeling that I know you from somewhere."

"Maybe you do."

"Well, what do we have here?" It was Joe Dunbar alongside Jason Steele coming up the boardwalk. "Looks like Preacher Boy is talking with Preacher Man."

Steele's black hat was pulled down low over his eyes and his usual coy smile was missing. He was clearly irritated by the wind. "Preacher, why don't you and Mr. Storeclerk there go inside and have a prayer meeting."

Boyd held Steele's hateful eyes. "*Then the beast was captured,*" he began, "*and with him the false prophet. And those two were cast into the lake of fire. And their army was slain by the one atop the horse.*" Boyd put an arm around Eli's shoulder and led him back inside the store.

Steele put a boot down on top of the pickle barrel. "Doing some shopping, I see. I thought that's what women were for."

"Are you two joined at the spurs?" Keene replied. "I've never seen you two more than ten feet apart. Don't you two get tired of each other? I've only been around you a week, and I'm already sick of you."

"I notice you travel alone," remarked Steele. "Kind of hard to watch your backside that way."

"That would be the way you would do it," Keene said. "You're not getting that ranch."

The comment inflamed Steele's temper. How dare this man tell him what he could or could not have? "What's going to stop me from taking it?" Steele said bitterly. "You? I've got more than thirty men, mister—and more if I want them. But I really don't think that many will be necessary.

"And after all this is over, who's going to be around to say Miss McKinnley didn't sell me the Bar MC, only to change her mind and try and take it back? It will be my word against yours . . . only you'll be dead. You think about that, mister. *I will have that ranch!"*

14

Adam LeFloure paced furiously, his boots clicking loudly in the heavy silence of the living room. With each passing day, he noticed Sarah becoming more at ease, more secure, despite her current situation.

"Sarah, I don't understand," Adam said. "There's no earthly reason for you to keep this ranch, especially when Steele could take it from you and you could end up with nothing but the clothes on your back—or maybe worse."

"Adam," Sarah replied, her voice strained. "I've also changed my mind about us."

"What are you saying?"

"I'm saying, I can't . . . I won't marry you."

"It's that gunman, isn't it?"

"He's not a gunman."

Adam stepped to Sarah, taking hold of her arms, almost as if he were scolding a child. "Do you honestly believe that man is going to be able to save this ranch for you?"

Sarah broke away. "You think that's why I don't want to marry you?"

"It's really quite clear, my dear." Adam was now wearing a spiteful grin. "You only wanted to marry me to get what you wanted, which at the time was to get back East. Now that your circumstances have changed, you need someone who serves your new interests best. It's only your good fortune that he's handsome. I know you never truly cared for me."

"That's not true."

"Come now, Sarah. If there's one thing I've learned about you, it's that the only person you truly care about is yourself."

Adam left, and Sarah found herself disappointed when he didn't slam the door on his way out.

Adam untied his dun and led it over to the water trough near the barn. The wind was stronger than that morning, kicking up dust in forceful gusts, making it at times difficult to see. Adam pulled out his handkerchief and doused it, while the dun drank. *God, it's hot*, Adam thought to himself.

Using the side of the barn as a windbreak, Adam leaned against the pine boards and wiped the wet handkerchief across his sweaty brow. He couldn't wait to leave this desolate place. He vowed right there never to come west of the Mississippi River again.

The shade of the barn offered some relief from the sun, and the wet handkerchief felt cool on his forehead. He was not looking forward to climbing back in the saddle. From inside the barn came voices, and he leaned in close to listen. He could hear Keene asking, "How far you figure it is to Ft. Tejon?"

"Probably close to a hundred miles," Pepper replied.

"What if I was to ride over there and bring the Army back?" Keene suggested. "You could gather up some of the other ranchers around the valley and hole up until I got back with the Cavalry. Maybe the Army could restore some order around here. At the very least they could look into McKinnley's murder and Steele's other dealings, and Sarah would be on record as to her position on selling the ranch should Steele try anything."

Pepper considered Keene's plan. He liked the idea of bringing in the Army. He also knew the government couldn't prosecute Steele unless they caught him in the act of something illegal. But it would definitely buy them some time.

"We couldn't hold out for long," Pepper remarked. "When you figure Steele to make his move?"

"Tomorrow at the earliest. I sense he threw out that threat so we could chew on it for awhile. My guess is he won't do anything for a couple of days."

"If you take the canyon, that would cut off close to forty miles," Pepper advised. "Course, you can't ride as fast in there what with all the rocks, but that roan of yours would be well rested when you come out the other side.

"If you leave before sundown and push hard, you could be at Ft. Tejon easily by sunup. That would put you back here . . . roughly, early tomorrow afternoon. But that's lightin' a fire under the army, and you know how those government types work."

Adam quietly backed away from the barn and stepped into the saddle of his dun. Any discomfort he was experiencing was lost with the information he now worked over in his mind.

He laughed to himself, then eased the dun into a gallop.

The sun was well down behind the Greenhorns when Pepper and Sarah set out from the ranch. The wind calmed with the setting sun, and in the west the last traces of light were fading from the darkening sky.

Pepper was not looking forward to what they were about to do.

Keene had left for Ft. Tejon two hours before, and now Pepper and Sarah were on their way to solicit help to keep Steele from following through with his threat to take the Bar MC by force. Pepper didn't like asking his friends to risk their lives. It was of no consequence to him that his friends had a stake in the outcome, or that if the situation were reversed he would be willing to do the same for them. It was different when he was doing the asking.

Sarah rode in the wagon, her mind still on Keene. She nearly ached inside when he was gone, and her heart raced when he was near. Was she falling in love with him? Sarah wasn't sure she was even capable of such an emotion. For Sarah, Keene's attraction began with the humble, confident style with which he carried himself. The composed manner he exuded and the controlled recklessness he could call up when the situation warranted. Keene was a man unlike any she had ever met.

Darkness covered the valley by the time Pepper and Sarah arrived at Jack Crawford's place. A yellow, gibbous moon illuminated the slanted roof, throwing a shadow of the two-room cabin across the dry ground.

Pepper knocked. It was several minutes before Ellen Crawford appeared. Pepper thought he could hear some arguing from inside, and his suspicion was confirmed when Ellen opened the door only wide enough to reveal her puffy, red frightened eyes. It was obvious she had been crying.

"Sorry to bother you this late, Ellen," Pepper apologized. "We need to talk to Jack, it's important."

Ellen Crawford glared out through the small opening in the door. "He can't help you," Ellen told them.

"For God-sakes, Ellen, let 'em in." It was Jack Crawford's pained voice calling out from the darkness. Reluctantly, Ellen pulled the door back to reveal her badly beaten husband.

Jack Crawford was shirtless, sitting in the shadows with his arm around Tommy. The small boy was teary eyed like his mother and he was clutching his father in fear and love. Crawford's ribs were bandaged, his face badly beaten and bruised. His nose was swollen to nearly twice its normal size.

Pepper burst into the darkened house. "My God, Jack, what happened to you?"

"A group of Steele's men came by about an hour ago," he groaned. "Said if I was to raise so much as a hand to help you, they'd be back, next time for my family."

Pepper put a hand on Crawford's shoulder. "Jack, I'm sorry."

"If I was twenty years younger . . ." Crawford's voice trailed off.

Sarah looked on from just inside the front door, attempting to avoid the scornful glare of Ellen Crawford. The stench of blood was heavy in the small cabin and, coupled with the site of an anguished Jack Crawford, it made Sarah feel sick to her stomach. She turned and started for the wagon.

"Where do you think you're going?" Ellen Crawford called out. Sarah turned back, a frail expression washed across her face. Never had she felt so exposed.

"You stay here and look at my husband, do you hear me?" Ellen Crawford was nearly yelling, and she was summoning up everything in her control not to completely break down. "You take a long, hard look Miss McKinnley, because this is all your fault!

"How dare you ride out here and ask for my husband's help. You told us selling your ranch was strictly business, remember? Well, let me tell you something, Miss McKinnley. You have no business here now, or ever again!"

Ellen Crawford's biting words were still haunting Sarah when she and Pepper arrived at Bob Powers' ranch a half-hour later. Powers limped out through the front door, using a rifle as a crutch. Like Crawford, Powers had been badly beaten. He cradled his tender ribs gently with his right arm.

"I've been expectin' you," Powers moaned. "Don't bother wastin' your time here, Pepper. Even if I wanted to help you, I'd be no good now." Then he added, "Steele's got you beat, I'm afraid."

"Dammit, Bob," Pepper cursed, "if Steele gets the Bar MC everyone loses, not just us."

"Face it Pepper, you've already lost. No one's gonna go up against Steele. You can't win."

Sarah was beginning to feel desperate. "Don't you people understand what's going to happen to you if Steele gets my ranch?"

Powers eyes narrowed. "Why the sudden concern for *us people*, Miss McKinnley? You sure didn't care about us last week, when you were gonna sell your ranch to Steele."

The night shadows brought on a sense of foreboding. Pepper and Sarah continued their bleak trek around the nearby ranches, finding out in each case that Steele's men had already been there. Pepper understood the beatings to be Steele's way of following up on his threat to Keene earlier that day, but what bothered him most was the feeling that Steele, somehow, seemed to know they would be coming. That part didn't make sense.

While Pepper reasoned, Sarah was on the verge of tears. Her world was crashing in upon her. For a quick moment she thought of Adam—perhaps she had been too hasty to dismiss him.

Sarah now resigned herself to the fact that no help would be offered her. She was alone in her fight against Steele and that realization, coupled with the hostility and resentment heaped on her this night, wore Sarah down.

Even more distressing to Sarah was the understanding that the animosity toward her was deserved. Not even Sarah could deny she had acted callously towards old family friends—friends of her father's since before she was born. It was a bitter pill to swallow.

She began to cry.

Pepper immediately brought the team to a stop. "Sarah, are you all right?"

"What do you think?" Sarah snapped. "These stupid people don't even care what's going to happen to us, or themselves."

"Sarah, you can't be upset at those folks for not throwin' in with us."

"Oh, yes I can!"

"For once in your life, Sarah, put yourself in someone else's boots. These people can't help us. If they do and we lose, not only would they probably be killed, but their families, too."

The tears began to sting Sarah's eyes. She brushed at them with the back of her hand. "So what you're telling me is they're looking out for themselves. How is that different from what I was doing?"

"They ain't got no choice," Pepper replied. "You did. No one was holding a gun to your head when you were gonna sell the ranch last week. Steele is putting a gun to theirs."

Sarah thought about Pepper's statement. As much as she did not want to admit it, he was right. "So, what do we do now?" she asked.

Pepper paused. "Pray that Keene makes it back with the Army before Steele comes."

Twenty-five miles away Keene was carefully picking his way through the rocky bottom of Kern Canyon.

The canyon's tall, sheer walls hid the moon from view and the dark shadows made seeing difficult. In a little over an hour, Keene would be free of the canyon and, except for the final twenty miles or so, would be riding over mostly flat farm land in the San Joaquin Valley. There he would be able to quicken the roan's pace. In less than three hours he would be at Ft. Tejon.

In an instant, the still night came alive by the dark figure of a man who emerged seemingly out of nowhere. The man tackled Keene off the roan and both men hit the ground hard.

Keene managed to struggle to his feet first. He didn't see the other man . . . or the rock that clubbed him over the head.

15

The man who struck Keene with the rock was Ivory, and it was his partner Reiger who knocked Keene out of the saddle. Deep claw marks were visible on both men's faces and arms, a sour memory of their tangle with the mountain lion, and each was looking for revenge.

Reiger tied Keene's hands behind his back and it took both men to heave Keene's body across the saddle of his roan. The two men were relieved knowing they would be back in Steele's good graces after their botched attempt to take Sarah three days previous. It was just past midnight when they swung into the front yard of Jason Steele's ranch—a multi-gabled fortress that matched the dark soul of its owner perfectly.

Inside, Steele sat behind a mahogany desk, puffing on a cigar; Joe sprawled in a seat across from him. They were discussing Keene, and were curious as to how no one had ever heard of this man before. Joe remarked that he had been unable to find any information at all on Keene. None of Joe's contacts had heard of him, and he could find no wanted posters on the man. It was as if Keene had no past, whatsoever. That seemed strange for a man of his boldness and abilities. The man was an enigma, and his mystery disturbed Steele.

Keene nearly fell when he was shoved into the red velvet-lined room.

"Well, who do we have here?" Steele said.

"He went through the canyon just like you said he would," Ivory commented.

"Of course, he did," Steele answered, taking a proud puff on the cigar he was working between his teeth. He looked at Keene and grinned. "Welcome to the Circle J— soon to be the largest ranch in the whole state of California."

"It's not going to work," Keene said with an air of confidence that annoyed Steele. "You're never going to get the Bar MC."

Steele stepped out from behind his desk. "I don't believe you are in a position to tell me what I will or will not be getting. By sundown tomorrow the Bar MC will be mine, and you, my friend, will be dead."

"Sarah's not going to trade me for her father's ranch," Keene said matter-of-factly.

"Then I'll just take it. That'll be the messy way of doing it, but I have a feeling Miss McKinnley will come around when she knows what the cards are." Steele smiled through the cigar. "From what I hear, she's taken quite a liking to you."

"You think you have it all figured out, don't you?" Keene replied.

Joe backhanded Keene across the mouth. "Don't be takin' that kind of attitude around here, Preacher Boy!"

"You know, Joe, my hands aren't always going to be tied. You're very brave when the odds are in your favor. Why don't you untie me and we'll see what kind of man you really are?"

Joe clenched his fist and gritted his teeth. He wanted to strike him again, but he knew doing that would only prove Keene's point. Joe was not a coward, but he did feel—although he would never admit it—that this man was his better. And as he had already experienced many times before with Keene, having the upper hand did not necessarily mean owning the advantage. For the moment Joe let Keene's challenge go, calling up a forged smile to mask his unsettled pride.

"Get him out of here!" Joe said to Reiger. "Tie him up in the barn." He leaned in close to Keene's face. "We ain't done yet, me and you. You made me look bad in front of a lot of my friends."

"I wouldn't lose any sleep over it, Joe," Keene replied. "I doubt you have that many friends to worry about."

Joe's face flushed red. Again, he turned to Ivory and Reiger. "Don't you two listen? I said, get him outta' here!"

Ivory yanked Keene around, prodding him out of the room with his pistol. When they were gone, Joe looked to Steele. "I'm gonna kill him."

Steele blew out a stream of white cigar smoke. "The second Sarah McKinnley signs over the deed, you can put a bullet through the back of his head, for all I care."

Escorted by Reiger, Ivory ushered Keene out of the main house, pushing and kicking him across to the yard to the barn. Keene fell twice, face first into the dirt, only to be jerked up, kicked from behind and pushed again.

Reiger pulled open the barn door. "Get in there!" Ivory commanded, kicking their prisoner inside.

Ivory shoved Keene down against a post. "Tie him up here."

Reiger grabbed a coil of rope from the wall. Out of the corner of his eye, he caught Ivory backhanding Keene across the face.

"Ivory!" Reiger shouted.

"I owed him that one," Ivory responded. He crowded his hairy face into Keene's. "Looks like your luck's done run out, mister. Just like Mr. Steele said, this time tomorrow, you'll be dead."

It was only hours before sun-up. A slight breeze rustled the curtains in Sarah's room, and the trees outside threw eerie shadows on her wall. She was having trouble sleeping and when she did sleep her dreams were dark and frightening. In a little over a week's time, Sarah had lost her father; nearly sold his ranch to the man who murdered him; alienated herself from most of her father's long-time friends; and met a man who made her feel things she had never felt before.

Sarah's mind skipped around like flies on a horse's tail—but always she found her thoughts returning to one thing . . . the man named Keene. Who was this man, really? And where was he right at this moment? He should be at Ft. Tejon by now, she gathered. And had she been rash when she told Adam she no longer wanted to marry him? True, she wasn't in love with him, but likewise, she couldn't say she was in love with Keene. Maybe she could learn to love Adam. If she had left with him a week ago, she would be far away from her problems now, on her way to a new life of luxury and fashion in the East.

For a moment, Sarah thought of bounding from the bed and riding into town to tell Adam she was sorry. Surely he would forgive her, and they could leave on the next stage out of Canaan Creek together. Then everything in Sarah's world would be right again. Something—Sarah didn't know what—kept her from doing this.

Another sleepless hour . . .

Sarah got out of bed and went downstairs. She was surprised to find Pepper cleaning a rifle by the fireplace.

"Can't sleep?" Sarah asked, falling into her father's chair.

"No—too many things on my mind."

"I feel like we've lost, Pepper." Sarah said gloomily. "Even if Keene gets back with the Army, it's probably only going to be a matter of time before Steele comes up with another plan to take the ranch. I feel like it's never going to end. Unlike my father, I just don't believe this ranch is worth dying for."

Pepper agreed. "You're right, Sarah. This ranch isn't worth dyin' for, and your father didn't think so, either. He didn't lose his life because of this ranch. He lost it because he refused to live his life in fear.

"When a person gives in to their fears, they're worse off than dead. That's not to say it's always easy to stand your ground, but running away from one's problems tends to become a habit. There's nothing wrong with being afraid to die, Sarah . . . just don't be afraid to live."

Sarah nodded. She had never thought of life in those terms.

Propping her head back against the armrest of the chair, Sarah closed her eyes to think more about Pepper's advice. The old chair felt safe and comforting, and with her eyes closed it was almost as if she were lying in her father's arms. She was drifting off to sleep when shots rang out from outside the house.

"Get down!" Pepper shouted, instinctively blowing out the lamp flame and dropping to the floor.

Sarah screamed and Pepper reached up and pulled her to the floor next to him. The gunshots resounded loudly and Sarah buried her head under her hands. Quickly Pepper realized that whoever was doing the shooting, they were not there to attack, for none of the bullets were hitting the house.

To Sarah it felt like an eternity, whereas in reality it was less than half-a-minute when the gunshots stopped.

In the silence that followed, Pepper could hear what he thought to be two, maybe three riders. They were talking, but he couldn't make out what they were saying. Then they stopped. More silence . . .

Sarah started to get up, but Pepper grabbed her wrist. "Stay down!" he whispered firmly.

A loud crash from the shattering window made Sarah scream again. Shouts and hollering followed from outside. Then the group of riders could be heard galloping off, their shouts slowly fading into the night. Sarah hugged the floor, her eyes clinched tightly. It was several moments before Pepper crawled his way over to the window to peak outside. The riders were gone.

"You can get up now," he said.

Sarah clung to the floor, her entire body trembling. "Sarah, are you hurt?" Pepper called.

"I'm selling this ranch, Pepper!" she said, her voice cracking. "This time I'm serious. I am selling this ranch and getting out of here!"

Pepper struck a match against the bottom of his boot and re-lit the lamp. Next to the table, he found the rock that had been thrown through the window.

"I can't take this anymore," Sarah continued. "I should have sold this place last week when I had the chance."

"Looks like that decision has already been made for you." Pepper was reading the piece of brown paper that had been tied around the rock. "Steele's got Keene. Says he'll be here one hour after sun-up to trade Keene for the deed to the ranch. Otherwise, he'll kill him and take the ranch by force."

16

Night dragged on towards morning. Inside the dimly lit barn, just steps away from Steele's main house, Keene remained tied with hands behind him to a post. Every once in a while Reiger or Ivory, who were standing guard, would look up from their card game and shoot him an irritable glance.

Once during the night Steele came in to look over his prisoner. He was barely able to contain himself now that the situation was again under his control. He reminded Keene that no man had ever called him a liar and lived to tell about it.

Steele had not planned to talk about his plans for the Bar MC, but in Keene's presence he found the need to gloat. Besides, the man would be dead in just a few hours. Steele had been carrying a secret with him for many years, and it was too good a secret to keep to himself. After the trouble this man had caused him, Steele wanted Keene to know he had been one step ahead of him the entire time. There was no denying Keene had won some battles, but Steele wanted to remind him it was he who was winning the war.

From the outset, Steele's scheme had been perfect. Although somewhat flawed in its execution—due mainly to Keene's unforeseen arrival—it was unerring in thought. Years before Jason Steele had ever set foot in the Kern River Valley his eyes were on it.

He bragged to Keene of the day that he overheard two business competitors talking about the possibility of gold in the Kern River Valley. His interest was piqued immediately. The two were thinking about investing in California gold ventures, but were hesitant at such a risky proposition. In 1880, it was believed that most of the gold had been mined out of California. Listening to the men talk while he ate his lunch alone in that Baltimore hotel restaurant, the seed was planted.

A man of considerable wealth from his dealings in the stock market, Jason Steele carried with him hidden aspirations for a career in politics. Low level political office did not interest him. Jason Steele wanted to be the governor of a state, and he did not think becoming President was out of the question. His ambitions were outmatched only by his self-confidence. However, his short temper and ruthless desire to win made him many enemies. He knew he would never be able to reach high political office in the East.

But in the West . . .

After lunch that day, Steele immediately began poring over maps of California he picked up at the Baltimore library. Within two months he would have maps of the Kern River Valley sitting open on his desk. He began studying the valley closely: its land, terrain, and history. Once Steele even made a trip to the Kern River Valley, but traveled in disguise so as not to be remembered. It was on that trip that Steele hired a man—only Steele was rich enough to afford this man—to go over the land to determine whether or not it concealed gold. The man was George Hearst who had made a fortune and a name for himself with a succession of mines, including the Homestake Gold Mine in Lead City, South Dakota. Hearst told Steele there was gold in the valley, but how much he could not say. He believed the main vein would be found along the Kern River. This accounted for Steele's obsession for the Bar MC which encompassed more of the Kern River than any ranch in the valley. Steele decided to act on Hearst's speculation. Hearst, after all, had built an empire on risk, along with acquiring an eventual seat in the United States Senate.

Steele bided his time, continuing to trade on the stock market, waiting for the perfect opportunity to make his move. While he waited, he continued to study the Kern River Valley, as well as California politics. He also learned to break and ride a horse. He even learned how to draw and shoot a Colt .45, becoming very proficient.

When the drought presented itself two years later, Steele seized the opportunity. He moved to the Kern River Valley and immediately began buying up land. The land would supply the gold, while the gold would give him the power he intended to ride to the Governorship of California and then to the Presidency of the United States of America.

Steele cared nothing for the cattle or the water. The stink he made over McKinnley's dam was strictly a diversion, a ruse to keep up his guise and urge things on to their eventual conclusion. He wanted the Bar MC strictly for its gold. He didn't care if it never rained in the valley again. That secret was partly responsible for the smugness that became a part of him. A plan that had begun over three years ago was now only hours away from being realized.

Steele was very pleased with himself when he finally left Keene, nearly an hour after he came to see him.

Daybreak loomed closer. Reiger and Ivory played cards to pass the time. They had gone nearly twenty-four hours without sleep and they were becoming irritable, even with each other.

"How did you two boys enjoy your lunch the other day?" Keene asked, breaking a long silence. "I hear mountain lion tastes *real* good."

Ivory tossed a card onto the bale of hay being used as a makeshift table. "Shut up!" he answered over his shoulder, "or we'll come over there and shut you up."

"Now you boys can't be roughing me up," Keene answered cheerfully. "Joe wouldn't like that. He wants me all to himself. I wouldn't be too upset, though. Consider those mountain lion scratches you got there character marks."

Ivory threw all his cards down this time. He stepped over and hovered threateningly over Keene.

"Could have been worse, you know," Keene went on. "That big cat probably didn't like the smell of tobacco."

"Don't listen to him," Reiger cautioned. "He's just tryin' to get atcha'."

"And it's working," Keene said. "So tell me, is mountain lion tough to chew on with only three teeth?"

Ivory smashed an uppercut into Keene's mouth.

Blood began to show on Keene's lips; still he held a wry grin. "Now that's real tough, hitting a man tied to a post. You weren't so tough when that mountain lion was staring you down though, were you? No sir, you were squawking for your mamma like a baby wanting milk."

Ivory drew out his .45, pressing it up against Keene's temple. "Shut up, right now!"

Reiger jumped to his feet. "Ivory!"

"Shoot me!" Keene defied him. "Come on, pull that trigger." Ivory cocked the .45 "Well, what are you waiting for?"

"Ivory, don't listen to him," Reiger said.

"Oh, he's listening," Keene said coolly. "And he knows he's not going to pull that trigger."

Ivory knew it too, and that rankled him even more.

Keene spurred him on. "Scared, ain'tcha? You know what Joe will do to you if you kill me. He wants that pleasure all to himself. So you might as well put that smoke-wagon away, because we both know you're not going to use it."

"You're pushin' it, mister," Reiger warned.

"You two just don't get it, do you? You can't threaten a dead man. You can only kill me once." Keene looked at Reiger. "Tell your partner here to holster that piece because we both know he's not going to use it. He's about as yellow as his teeth."

"All right, mister! You want me, you got me!" Ivory shoved the .45 back in the holster. "I may not be able to kill you, but I'm gonna hurt you real bad."

He spit out some of his chew and began to untie Keene.

Reiger grabbed his shoulder. "You can't do that!"

"Get back!" Ivory shouted, throwing off Reiger's grip.

"What about Steele?" Reiger reminded him. "And Joe!"

"I don't care! No one calls me yellow without consequences. Go outside and keep an eye out. I'm gonna teach this boy some manners. If he's a little beat up when Joe comes to get him, I'll tell him our prisoner got a little unruly."

Reiger hesitated. He didn't like it, but he understood Ivory wanting to get even.

"Go on." Ivory said roughly. Finally, Reiger nodded his agreement and stepped outside.

Ivory resumed untying Keene. He slipped out the last knot, then moved back quickly. As Keene rose to his feet, Ivory kicked him with his boot toe. It was a cheap shot, but effective, catching Keene on the chin and sending him toppling back to the ground.

Outside, Reiger stood watch, nervously smoking a cigarette while he waited. Every few moments his eyes would go to the main house, which was completely dark except for a faint light that filtered out from deep within.

The air was cool and it felt good to be outside the stuffy barn. Far off in the east, he could see the first traces of light separating from the darkness. It would be daylight soon.

Grunts and groans seeped out through the crack in the barn doors, and Reiger could hear Ivory barking at Keene, although he couldn't make out exactly what he was saying. Physically, Reiger knew Ivory was no match for the younger, more fit man. But Reiger also knew of no one who could equalize their odds by fighting dirty better than Ivory. He had watched Ivory best men twice his size without ever taking a punch.

Taking another drag on his cigarette, something caught Reiger's attention in the direction of the main house. To his dismay, it was Joe coming off the last step. He was on his way to the bunkhouse to get the men started. Joe appeared hollow-eyed and worn, but he was looking forward to this day. Once they had the Bar MC and he finished off Keene, his life was going to become much more leisurely.

Joe headed straight for Reiger who was crushing out his cigarette, doing his best to act natural. To Reiger's relief, the sounds of fighting from inside the barn had stopped.

"What are you doing out here?" Joe grunted.

"Nothin'," Reiger answered. "Just came out for some air."

"You got it," Joe replied shortly. "Now get back inside."

Joe started again for the bunkhouse. The loud clang of a shovel brought his attention back to the barn.

"What the hell was that?" Joe demanded to Reiger.

Both men sprang inside the barn where it was quiet and dark. On the ground they found Ivory, sprawled in unconscious sleep next to the shovel that put him there. A kerosene lamp lay broken a few feet away and flames were beginning to catch on the hay-covered floor. Reiger grabbed up a nearby pail of water and doused the fire.

Joe was incensed. "What's goin' on Reiger?"

"He was making fun of Ivory," Reiger explained. "Ivory untied him, so he could fight him." He observed Ivory's limp body. "I guess he lost."

"That's the second time this week you two have botched things up," Joe fumed. "There won't be a third."

Joe drew his Colt and peered through the dark shadows of the barn. "He's still in here," he said, loud for Keene's benefit, "and the only way out is through us."

He pointed with his Colt for Reiger to cover one side of the barn. Reiger drew his .45 and stepped into the darkness.

Shadows made odd shapes along the walls, giving both men an unsettling feeling. They stepped cautiously, their six-shooters cocked and ready, making their way toward the back wall.

An old coach, a leftover from the previous owners of the ranch, sat discarded off to Reiger's left. It was covered in layers of dust and leaned to one side where a front wheel was broken.

Tentatively, Reiger edged up to the coach's side door. He yanked open the padded door, leading with his .45.

The coach was empty and Reiger, somewhat relieved, slammed the door shut. Out of the darkness, a hand reached out and jerked him back by the collar.

Joe heard Reiger grunt, followed by the dull sound of fist hitting bone. In the split second it took Joe to spring across from his side of the barn, Keene, like a phantom, had vanished into the shadows.

Joe jumped back to the center of the barn.

Now that he was alone, he was uneasy. "I'm gonna find you eventually, Preacher Boy!" Joe called out. Deep down, he wasn't sure he wanted to.

Joe stepped lightly, listening intently for any sound, any trace of movement. He had heard of Indians who were so quiet of foot they could actually sneak up on a man in the dark and be standing next to him, without giving away their position. Joe wasn't scared, but he was nervous. Once again, Keene had stolen the edge.

Now nearing the back of the barn, Joe felt his heart speeding up. In front of the back wall a stack of hay bales formed a barrier, behind which sat four wooden crates. If Keene weren't hunkered down behind the crates, he would have to be in the loft.

Joe's finger pulled tighter against the trigger, making him feel more secure, more confident. The shadows were darker here, but his eyes were beginning to adjust. He kicked his way through the bales of hay and stepped to the crates leading with his gun . . . Keene wasn't there.

"Looks like it's just you and me now." It was Keene's voice behind him.

Joe wheeled. "So, it is."

Keene stepped forward and Joe brought up his .45. "No, you stay right there."

"You seem to be awfully nervous to be the one holding the gun," Keene said.

"You always got something cute to say, don't you, Preacher Boy." Then Joe added, "I ain't afraid of you."

"You saying that for my benefit or yours?"

Joe smiled, but it wasn't friendly. No living man had ever talked to Joe like this; the ones who had were now dead. Joe wasn't lying, he wasn't afraid of Keene, but the man did throw off Joe's guard.

"Alright, Preacher Boy," Joe said, holstering the Colt. "I beat you within an inch of your life once—I can do it again."

He threw up his fists and began to circle Keene, sizing him up, looking for an opening.

"I'm gonna prove to you that I ain't afraid," Joe said, then he threw a wild punch that Keene easily avoided.

"You're going to have to do better than that, Joe," Keene said smiling.

This time Joe lunged for him, leading with his right. Keene caught the punch with his left palm, and came back with a right of his own, that caught Joe on the side of the lip. It cut him and Joe stepped back, spitting blood.

Joe's eyes were angry now and again he came at Keene. He feigned with his right, and then struck quickly with a left jab that landed just under Keene's right eye. It knocked him backward, but he kept to his feet.

"Good one, Joe."

"You got lucky out on the street that day," Joe said sourly.

This time Joe feigned with his right and swung with a roundhouse left. It was swift and powerful, and when it missed Joe was thrown off balance. Keene stepped up and landed a left to the side of Joe's face. Joe went down hard, toppling over the short wall of hay, falling into the wooden crates behind.

In the fall Joe lost his hat, and his straggly hair now mixed with strands of hay. "Joe, you're lucky those friends of yours can't see you now."

Keene's quick wit cut like his punches. Joe gritted his teeth, full of hate. He spun around on his knees, making a play for his gun, but Keene stepped up and kicked the six-shooter out of Joe's hand as he drew. The .45 disappeared somewhere under the hay.

"What's wrong, Joe? Don't have a saloon full of friends to help you out this time?"

Joe lunged up at Keene, yelling as he came. Keene, easily the more able-bodied of the two, jumped quickly to the side. As Joe went by, Keene kicked him in the seat of the pants, sending him face down to the ground.

"Don't get up, Joe. You're where you belong, on your belly like the snake you are."

Joe sprang to his feet. The sweat on his face was mixed with blood, and his eyes were wild and crazy. He looked and acted like a madman.

"I'm gonna kill you!" Joe yelled, taking a wild, useless swing which Keene was able to duck easily. This continued for several moments, Joe's movements now having no focus or direction. Joe was tiring from violent anger and flailing punches. Finally, Keene returned a missed punch with a short, powerful blow to Joe's ribs. The air left Joe's lungs and he collapsed, gasping for breath.

"You're done, Joe. Face it, without your guns or someone to back you up, you're not worth much."

Joe was on his knees, coughing; attempting to catch his breath. When it returned he came at Keene again. His hate and pride would not allow him to quit.

He flailed at Keene, who kept him at arm's length, and when Joe tired, barely able to lift his fists, Keene stepped up landing an uppercut squarely under Joe's chin. The punch lifted Joe off his feet, sending him toppling over the bales of hay.

Joe groaned and then his sweaty body went limp. He was out cold, an arm resting across the top of a wooden crate marked in big, bold letters on the side: **DYNAMITE.**

17

The Steele ranch was quiet while dawn set to bloom behind the eastern Sierra peaks. In moments the coming sunrise would stir the ranch back to life and Steele men would be rousing in the bunkhouse.

Inside the barn, groans from the three beaten men mixed with the smell of hay and grain. Keene stepped over Joe and went right to work. He grabbed an empty dried oats sack from a nail off the wall, and then removed Joe's hand from the top of the crate. Joe moaned but it would be several minutes before he would be able to get to his feet.

Working quickly with no wasted moves, Keene began stuffing the sack with sticks of dynamite, their caps and fuses already in place. When the bag was full, he stepped back over Joe and started for outside.

He paused to peek between the crack in the two big doors . . . the yard was quiet. Keene dashed across to the corral and climbed over the rail. Steele's remuda of horses moved nervously about him as he attempted to herd them to the front of the corral. Once the horses were where he wanted them, Keene began placing sticks of dynamite under the back fence in ten-foot intervals.

He struck a match, lit the first stick and then moved swiftly to the second. He was lighting the third and final stick, when a shirtless man came through the bunkhouse door. It was Clay Donnally wiping the sleep from his eyes.

"Hey, what the hell do you think you're doin'?" Clay called out. When it registered, he started in a dead run for Keene, who was now headed for the roan still tied up outside the main house.

Clay was coming off the bunkhouse porch when the first stick detonated. The deafening explosion reverberated out with a flash of yellow light, lifting Clay off his feet and sending him crashing back against the adobe wall.

The bone jarring blast brought men scurrying out of the bunkhouse. They were throwing on shirts and pulling up pants, streaming out off the porch when the second stick ignited.

Steele was outside the main house before the third explosion. He came out the front door just in time to meet Keene mounting the roan, the sack of dynamite flung over his shoulder. Steele went for his gun, but he wasn't wearing it.

Keene smiled. "I told you, you're not getting that ranch." And he was off atop the roan, disappearing in a haze of confusion and smoke.

Steele looked out angrily at the frightened horses. He could do nothing but watch helplessly as his entire remuda stampeded over and through the front gate of the corral, out into the red glowing sky of morning.

Pepper couldn't believe his eyes when he saw Keene coming through the front door of the house.

"How'd you get away from Steele's?" Pepper said, Keene's presence energizing him.

"Later—where's Sarah?"

Pepper explained how Sarah had handed him the deed to the ranch shortly after Steele's men tossed the rock message through the window. Then she had hurried out on her father's appaloosa. "I think she went to find Adam," Pepper said.

"Meet us up at the reservoir in two hours," Keene told him. "I got an idea how we can save this ranch."

A clear blue dominated the morning sky. It was warm and Sarah was perspiring when she dismounted outside the Canaan Creek Hotel. She pushed through the front doors, hurried across the empty lobby, and climbed the stairs with purposeful determination.

After several frantic knocks, which echoed in the quiet hallway, Adam LeFloure opened the door.

"Well, well . . . isn't this indeed a surprise," Adam remarked, his smile rich with sarcasm.

Sarah was frenzied. "I was afraid you might already be gone."

"If you must know, I'll be leaving this poor excuse for a town on the noon stage—but let's not discuss this in the hallway."

Adam continued as he closed the door. "You must pardon me if I'm a little troubled by your sudden concern for my whereabouts."

Sarah glanced at the open suitcase on the bed. "Adam, I'm sorry! I didn't mean all those things I said. I was confused."

"Am I to assume you're talking about the part of not wanting to marry me?"

Sarah swept up close to him and Adam could smell the sweet scent of her perfume. "I didn't mean that!" she said. "So much was happening, I didn't know what to think or feel. Please, Adam, take me with you."

"Really, Sarah, groveling doesn't become you at all."

"I'm sorry, Adam! I've never said that before in my life."

"That, my dear, I would believe to be true."

"Give me another chance, Adam." Sarah pleaded. She felt desperate, with no shame. "Don't you think I'm worth it?"

Temptation was now beginning to grab hold of Adam. His weakness had always been beautiful women. But then, maybe that wasn't a weakness after all, he thought.

"What about your man, Keene?" Adam said. "Are you tossing him away now that Steele has him?"

His comment surprised her. "How did you know about that?"

"Small town," Adam replied. "Information has a way of making the rounds. That is why you're here, isn't it?" He laid a folded shirt in the suitcase and closed it.

"No, I never loved Keene. I told you, I was confused."

Adam considered Sarah's appeal for a moment. There were few things about her he found to admire. She was a weak woman, really, who would do anything or say anything to get what she wanted. But she was beautiful.

Her smooth complexion, perfect lips, the blonde hair . . . yes, that could be enough for Adam to overlook her selfish character—for a time. He would use her just as she had used him. And when he was done with her, he would discard her like one of his old silk shirts.

It was ironic, Adam thought to himself. An acquaintance of Steele's, Adam had come out from Philadelphia to gain inside information on John McKinnley through Sarah. Steele had gambled on Sarah falling for Adam, but knowing Adam's charm with women and Sarah's strong desire for an Eastern man, it was a calculated risk. It was no accident when Adam stepped in Sarah's path from the darkened doorway of the hotel, and she had taken the bait like a hungry bear.

Adam had never entertained any notion of marrying Sarah. He was simply going to slip out of town the minute the ranch was sold to Steele. Adam had come to Canaan Creek, earned his five thousand dollars, and was now leaving with the trick.

"Alright, you can come," Adam finally said. "We leave at noon."

Sarah was beaming when they exited the hotel. "I won't be long," she promised.

Adam helped her up onto the appaloosa. It was already hot out on the street and Adam couldn't wait to be rid of Canaan Creek.

"You won't regret this," Sarah said happily.

Adam smiled—not at her comment, but at his secret. "Alright, my dear, just make sure—" Adam stopped short. His smile withdrew and his eyes grew timid and wide.

"What's wrong?" Sarah asked.

She turned in the direction Adam was facing. Keene was riding up on the roan.

"Keene!" Sarah called out, excitement and relief in her voice.

Adam stiffened and his eyes held Keene's.

"You're hurt?" Sarah said, noticing the black eye Keene was sporting from Joe's punch.

"Oh, it's nothing," he replied. "Sarah, If you want to keep your father's ranch you have to come with me right now."

"But we've got no help."

"Sarah, we don't need help." Keene outlined his plan to blow up the French Gulch Bridge when Steele and his men rode across to come out and take the Bar MC.

"What if he doesn't come that way?"

"He will," Keene replied confidently. "His only other choice is to go the long way up the riverbed, but Steele's too impatient for that. I ran off his horses. When he comes, he's going to come fast and angry."

She envisioned Keene's plan. From the moment she saw him, Sarah had forgotten completely about Adam, along with everything she had told him up in the hotel room.

Adam turned and walked away.

"Adam?" Sarah called, but he didn't turn around. "Adam? Adam, where are you going?"

He was gone, withdrawing back inside the hotel.

18

Jason Steele was breathing fire. "How long before we get those horses back?"

"Probably a couple of days," Joe Dunbar answered, sore and squinting through a swollen left eye. "Those explosions scared 'em pretty good."

"You let me know the minute we get 'em back." Steele pounded his fist hard on the desk. "I'm getting that ranch and that gold!"

"For another five thousand dollars, I can tell you how to do that without getting yourself blown up." It was Adam LeFloure sauntering into the room.

Steele turned back to Joe. "Is there anything else?"

"No."

"Then I suggest you get back out there and find those horses."

Joe was seething as he left and he couldn't wait to take it out on Ivory and Reiger.

Steele seated himself behind his desk. "What are you still doing around here?" he said to Adam. "I already paid you your money, and for what? A little information I could have picked up on my own."

"I had that ranch handed to you, until that Keene character showed up." Adam helped himself to a cigar from the box on the desk. "As a matter of fact, he's the reason I'm here now. I just ran into him in town. Seems he's got a surprise picked out for you."

"And what surprise might that be?"

Adam struck a match against the arm of the chair. "That, my friend, is going to cost you."

"You already got your pay. You're not getting a dollar more from me."

"Come now, Jason," Adam said, lighting his cigar. "Isn't your life worth a paltry five thousand dollars, especially to a rich man like yourself?"

Steele knew that it was. After a moment of consideration, he moved to the safe behind the desk. "This better be good," he grunted.

Adam puffed on the cigar. "Oh, it is."

A faint breeze sifted through the valley, rustling the leaves of the dry oaks and taking the edge off a hot day. Sitting their mounts overlooking the McKinnley dam, Keene, along with Pepper and Sarah, awaited the coming storm. Pepper was pleased to have Keene back, but he wondered if perhaps the inevitable was only being delayed.

While Pepper and Keene talked, Sarah sat half-listening, her mind in a perpetual state of confusion. She had run back to Adam out of fear, attempting to regain something that was never there. When Keene showed up her heart jumped, and she immediately forgot all about Adam. Life was hitting Sarah from all sides. She was very confused.

"How long you figure before Steele comes?" Pepper asked.

"They're going to be busy rounding up those horses at least until tomorrow," Keene said.

"And then what?"

Sarah perked up. "He's going to blow up the French Gulch Bridge when Steele and his men come across." She looked at Keene, waiting for him to fill in the rest.

"Actually, Sarah, that was only for Adam to hear," Keene said.

Sarah's forehead crinkled; she didn't understand. Was anything what it seemed anymore?

"Adam is working for Steele," Keene informed her. "I heard his name mentioned last night at Steele's place."

"I'll be damned," Pepper commented. "I always thought there was something sneaky about that man. So many things didn't seem to add up."

Adam working for Steele?

Sarah didn't want to believe it. But the more she thought about it, the more it made sense. Adam had tried to push her into selling her father's ranch from almost the moment she first met him. The thought of how close she actually came to selling out to Steele made her shiver. She felt foolish, angry, and embarrassed.

"So, what's this about blowing things up?" Pepper asked, getting the subject back on track.

Keene briefly outlined his plan. They all agreed they could not shoot it out with Steele—he simply had too many men. Keene's idea was to strike in a place where Steele and his men would all be concentrated in one area. A place like a bridge or, better yet, the riverbed. They could blow up the dam, sending a wall of water right down on top of Steele and his men.

"I made it very clear to Adam that we were expecting Steele to come over the bridge," Keene said. "The only option left is the riverbed."

Pepper mulled over Keene's plan. The strategy was risky, but options for them right now were as few as raindrops. The only thing they could count on would be Steele's impatience. That would definitely work in their favor. Pepper liked Keene's plan, but looking out over the calm water of the half-filled reservoir he became troubled.

"What is it?" Sarah asked.

Pepper rubbed his chin. "If Steele does come up the riverbed, I don't know that there's enough water in that reservoir to do the job."

"Pepper's right!" Sarah exclaimed. "Look how low the water is, and where are we going to find more water in the middle of a drought? She became distressed. "I can't believe this is happening to me!"

"Sarah—" Keene said, but she continued on.

"What was I thinking? We can't beat Steele!"

"Sarah."

"What are we going to do?"

"SARAH!"

Keene's bold eyes leveled in on her and she understood right then; he did have an answer to the burning question, he had not overlooked the obvious.

With the utmost certainty, Keene said simply, "It's going to rain."

19

A strong wind blew down over the Greenhorn Mountains and out across the dry valley. The blades of dead grass bent with the strong gales, and where there was no grass, dirt kicked up into swirling dust devils. There had been only a trace of a breeze when Pepper arrived at the dam to meet Keene and Sarah, and now, nearly an hour later, they all struggled to keep their hats on their heads.

They led their mounts down from the reservoir into the Kern River bed, not far from where Sarah had encountered the mountain lion. How very long ago that seemed to her now, when it had actually been less than a week. She felt she had lived three lifetimes since her father's death.

If one good thing had come of all this, it was that Sarah had found a deeper respect for her father. She had only been living his life for a few days, and already she was spent from the responsibility. How tired he must have been . . . and sad. Fighting Steele everyday, running a ranch in the middle of a drought, and raising a feisty daughter left its mark, but he never let it show. Her father greeted each day, each person, with the same cheerful expression.

Sarah couldn't do that. She was tired and irritable, and when she thought again of Keene's prediction of rain, she began to get angry.

How could this man be so arrogant as to predict rain? And how could he stake their lives on something that had not happened in over two years?

There must be another way, some better plan even if she couldn't come up with it. Again, Sarah thought of Adam. Life for Sarah always seemed better in retrospect.

Keene stopped the roan. "This is the place," he instructed Pepper. "You'll be hidden in the trees, and when Steele and his men get to this point, you fire off a couple of shots in the air. That'll give me the signal to blow the dam."

Pepper nodded in agreement while Sarah continued to brood. She pulled her hat string tighter to keep the wind from blowing the hat off her head.

"Is there an old abandoned mine shaft around here?" Keene asked.

"A few hundred feet downstream," Pepper pointed. "Well, downstream if there was a river."

"Steele believes there's gold there," Keene said.

His comment puzzled Sarah. "Gold? On this land?"

Keene recounted Steele's late-night confession. He also told them of the mineshaft Steele mentioned that Sarah's father had built. "Steele believed that your father knew the ranch contained gold and that's why he was so reluctant to sell."

The mineshaft Steele spoke of was, in actuality, a crude hole, roughly eight feet across and fifteen feet deep. It burrowed into a small incline located about fifty yards from the riverbed. Arriving at the site, they found fresh dirt and picks scattered about the opening.

"It looks like someone's been messing around here," Pepper noted.

"My father never talked about any gold on this land." Sarah was incredulous. "If there were any, wouldn't he have mined it out? We would have been rich." Sarah enjoyed the prospect of the thought. "He could have sent me to school."

"There's always been speculation that this land held a great deal of gold," Pepper said. "John and I started that shaft ourselves, but then John changed his mind. He decided he was already what he wanted to be—a rancher. He had no desire to be rich. He practically was already. What he didn't want was every damn fool who did want to get rich coming in and digging up his land."

Sarah couldn't believe it. "You mean the money to send me to school is right there in that hole?"

"It's not that easy, Sarah," Pepper replied. "You don't just reach in and grab it. Putting in a mining operation would have changed the entire landscape of the ranch. And gold isn't something that's easy to keep a secret. This entire valley would have been overrun by golddiggers.

"Your father didn't want the headache, and maybe you don't understand this, but there's more to life than just money. Like I said before, your father wanted to be a rancher, not a mine owner."

Sarah couldn't comprehend that logic. For her, life was about dollars and cents, wanting and having. But a change was happening in Sarah. Where before she would have dismissed her father's rationale if it differed from her own, this time she tried to look at it from his point of view. Maybe she couldn't fully understand it, but for the first time she at least considered it.

"Don't you think it would be a good idea if one of us rode out to check up on Steele?" Keene suggested. "Just to see how he's coming along with those horses."

Pepper agreed and offered to go, but Sarah was still holding on to something.

"Wait a minute," she said. "What are we going to do when Steele comes? Surely you weren't serious about relying on the rain to save us." Sarah turned pleadingly to Pepper. "Please tell me we have something better to risk our lives on."

Pepper had nothing to offer her and while it bothered him also, there was something in the way the words rolled off Keene's lips with such certainty that made Pepper want to believe.

"Sarah," Pepper began, "I don't know if it's gonna rain or not, but even though there's a mighty slim chance, it's the only chance we got—and that's better than no chance at all, which is what we had before. You know I'm not a religious man like your father, but I'll tell you what, I'll be prayin' for rain like I never prayed for nothin' else." He smiled over at Keene. "Hell, I've already started."

"You're going to get us killed," Sarah said, looking at Keene.

Keene sidestepped his roan up alongside Sarah. "How do you know it's not going to rain? As much as you think

I'm wrong, why can't I be just as right? You say I can't guarantee rain, but can you guarantee, beyond the shadow of a doubt, it's not going to rain?"

"This is absurd!" Sarah said flustered. "It hasn't rained here in two years."

"And that means it's never going to rain again?"

"Not today it's not! You're just like my father. Faith on Sundays is one thing, but it's not going to stop Steele from shooting us full of holes."

"Sometimes faith is all people have to go on," Keene said earnestly, "and most of the time they come to find out, it's all they really needed."

Sarah returned to the Bar MC with Keene, while Pepper rode off to check on Steele. Nothing more was mentioned of Keene's prediction of rain. Upon returning to the ranch, Sarah, fatigued from thought and no sleep from the night before, fell immediately across her bed. She was asleep in minutes.

All afternoon Sarah slept a deep, restful sleep, while outside a steady wind continued to blow out of the east. On the wind came clouds; large, gray clouds piled high atop one another, rising all the way up into the heavens. The menacing clouds seemed to converge from all directions, moving ominously and gathering together like an army heading into battle. Slowly, they overtook the retreating sun and darkness enveloped the Kern River Valley. The wind then calmed and the air fell eerily silent.

Sarah awoke to find her room dark. A voice brought her out of her peaceful slumber, and as she slowly gathered her senses, she thought it to be evening. Sarah stretched, feeling rested for the first time in quite a while.

Again, she heard the voice, and now she could make out that it was Pepper. He was yelling up at her and the excitement in his voice could only mean one thing: *Steele was coming!*

Fully awake now, Sarah bounded from the bed and threw open the window, pushing her head outside.

She found Pepper down below, dancing out in the yard with his arms spread open wide.

"Pepper Martin, have you gone crazy?" Sarah hadn't noticed the small bead of water that had landed on her forehead, or the tiny wet drops falling around her.

A loud roll of thunder boomed overhead, echoing across the valley and out over the mountaintops.

Peering up into the purple-gray sky, Sarah now realized it was not evening at all. Storm clouds obscured the late afternoon sun and it was beginning to *rain*.

20

The people of Canaan Creek—what few were left—congregated in the streets, dancing, crying, and sharing with one another in the glorious wet rain. The big drops brought joy to the people, releasing the hopelessness pent up inside them for nearly two years. Their prayers had been answered, and once again Canaan Creek was full of promise, just as it had been in the times before the long drought, before Jason Steele. With arms and happy faces uplifted towards the heavens, the people gathered to celebrate the gift from Above. And like blood to a dying patient, the rain brought back life to the Kern River Valley.

"Isn't it wonderful!" cried a woman.

"It's a miracle," another woman answered, baby in arms.

"I hope it never stops!" a man shouted gleefully.

"Damn rain!" cursed Jason Steele.

To Steele the rainfall was nothing more than an irritant. Steele's thoughts centered strictly on rounding up his horses as soon as possible, and then riding immediately out to take the Bar MC. He wanted the gold on McKinnley land and the rain was just another obstacle in his way. He was not happy to see Joe riding into the yard without the horses.

The rest of the men followed Joe. A few on horseback, some in wagons, and the rest in soggy boots. As one man, they made a direct line for the comforts of the dry bunkhouse. Joe trotted his bay over to the porch to report to his boss.

"What are you doing back?" Steele shouted through the rain. "You can't get those horses if you're all here at the ranch."

"It's getting dark, and it's starting to rain harder." Joe answered, looking for sympathy where there was none. "We weren't dressed for it."

"You go tell those men, I said to get their butts back out there. I don't want to see one man here at the ranch until every one of those damned horses is rounded up. Do you understand me?"

Joe glared at his boss. He was wet, tired, and hungry. And he was looking forward to a cup of coffee that now would have to wait. He jerked the bay around and headed for the bunkhouse, cursing up at the wet sky, "Damn rain."

The valley grew darker and soon it would be nightfall. What had begun as a light sprinkle of rain was now a steady downpour that would continue into the night.

While Joe and his men headed back out to find more horses, Pepper and Keene inspected the dam. The water level of the reservoir was rising and the rain had become so heavy Pepper couldn't see the pine trees lining the other side.

"It hasn't rained this hard in ten years," Pepper stated. "I just hope it takes Steele awhile to get those horses rounded up."

"We'll be alright," Keene said. "This rain isn't making it any easier on them. It should keep 'em busy a little while longer."

Pepper pulled his rain slicker tighter. "What about that dynamite you're plannin' to use? Those fuses are mighty long. They're liable to get washed out, don't you think?"

"I'll just cut' em down."

"That's not gonna give you much time to get out of there before they blow."

"It'll be alright." Keene said it with the same conviction as his prediction of the rain.

Pepper turned his mount. "By the way, where did you manage to come up with all that dynamite?

Keene grinned. "Steele donated it."

It was after midnight when Joe and his men returned with the remaining horses. They were exhausted, and each was looking forward to dry clothes and most of all, sleep.

Clay Donnally rode up next to Joe, while the rest of the men herded the horses into the busted corral and fashioned a makeshift picket line.

"I can't wait to get out of this rain and grab me a hot cup of coffee," Clay said.

Joe didn't feel like talking. "I better go tell Steele we're back."

He sloshed into the house to find Steele eating a late meal at his desk. "We got the horses back," he reported.

"Good!" Steele answered through a mouthful of steak. "Have the men get saddled up and ready to ride."

"Now?"

Steele wiped at the corners of his mouth with a cloth napkin. "Yes, now."

All Joe could think of was his warm bed. "We were out all night!" Joe looked longingly at the fried potatoes and the half-eaten steak on Steele's plate. "The men are tired, not to mention hungry."

Steele slurped his hot coffee. "That doesn't concern me at the moment. I want that ranch and I want that gold. As soon as I have both, the men can eat until they're fat and sleep until they're dead."

Steele finished his meal. Fifteen minutes later when he exited the house, he found a surly group of men waiting for him. The rain was still coming down in hard sheets and it stung when it hit the flesh. Steele pulled his hat down low on his head and adjusted his yellow poncho, before he stepped into the saddle.

"I don't see why we have to do this now," Ivory complained from the back. "I think he's gone crazy."

Steele jerked around, drawing his pistol as he turned. He fired off one shot, catching Ivory in the chest and knocking him from the saddle. Ivory was dead before he hit the mud.

"It was his fault we had to do it this way," Steele said, addressing his men. "If anyone else has any objections, I'll be glad to oblige you." None of the men spoke up, although all of them objected. Steele holstered his .45. "Alright then, let's ride!"

For hours Sarah watched the rain through the window, as if in a trance, ruminating of Keene and his prediction. She knew no more of him now than the first time she had laid eyes on him. Sarah didn't like not knowing things; it made her feel vulnerable.

She could hear Keene stamping off his muddy boots on the porch boards before entering the house. "I'm going to relieve Pepper," he told her.

"Who are you?" she asked. "No one . . . no one can do the things you do. It's been raining almost from the moment you said it would."

Pepper's excited voice and clumping boots on the porch put their conversation on hold. He bolted into the house, dripping wet and nearly out of breath. "Steele's on his way," he informed them.

Sarah's eyes remained on Keene. "You're never going to tell me are you?"

"When this is all over, you'll find out everything you want to know."

"Is that a promise?"

"It's a promise."

21

Steele and his men rode hard and determined through the harsh, driving rain. At times, thunder boomed so close the men would flinch in their saddles. They were worn and tired from retrieving the horses, but they followed their leader obediently across the water-soaked meadows of the Kern River Valley.

Out of the west hills, a rider approached. He could only be seen every few minutes when lightning cracked, lighting up the night sky as if it were day. When the rider got close, Steele threw up a gloved hand bringing his men to a stop in unison behind him.

The loan rider reined in and threw back his hooded poncho—it was Adam LeFloure.

"What the hell are you doing out here?" Steele yelled through the downpour.

"The road is flooded through the canyon so they cancelled my stage," LeFloure answered. "I thought since I'm condemned to spend more time here, I would ride out to see if you had taken over the Bar MC. I assume that is where you are headed now?"

"The Bar MC will be mine within the hour," Steele boasted, the thought removing the irritation of the rain for a brief moment. "What's it to you?"

"Consider it personal," Adam replied. "Care if I ride along to watch?"

"Be my guest," Steele grunted. "Just make sure you don't get in the way."

Adam pulled his poncho back over his head. "I see you're taking the long way around."

"Can't be too careful," Steele replied grimly.

At that same moment, Keene was waiting calmly up at the McKinnley dam. Back at the Bar MC, he had cut down the fuses on the dynamite sticks to the length of his middle finger before tying the sticks with a leather thong in bundles of seven and eight. When he arrived at the dam, he wedged the bundles of dynamite deep into the rocks, covering them as best he could to keep the sticks and fuses dry. He spread the bundles out, roughly twenty feet apart, then settled down on his haunches under the roan.

Out of the blanket of rain, Sarah appeared atop her father's appaloosa.

"What are you doing here?" Keene demanded, coming out from under the roan.

Sarah was soaked, her blonde hair matted against the front of her face underneath her poncho. "I couldn't sit back at the ranch and do nothing. I was going crazy."

"This is no place for you, Sarah," Keene said severely. "Go back to the ranch, right now."

"Let me stay!" Sarah pleaded. "I'll be safe with you."

"Sarah, I don't want you anywhere close to here when that dynamite goes off."

"What about you? I can help."

"No! Sarah, I'll be all right. Now get back to the ranch. There's nothing you can do here but get yourself killed."

Reluctantly Sarah rode off, but with no intention of going back to the Bar MC. She couldn't sit idly by, letting her future be determined for her. No, she must have a hand in deciding her fate, whatever the consequences.

From the moment Keene sent her away, Sarah began forming her own plan. She would ride downstream, past where Pepper was staked out, and watch for Steele herself. Once she caught sight of Steele and his men, she would ride back and alert Keene. She hoped to arrive before Pepper fired off his warning shots, so she could help Keene light the fuses. She had been worrying about the short fuses and Keene's safety ever since Pepper had voiced his concern. Maybe she could make a difference.

The rain continued to fall in heavy sheets, sending out a continuous high-pitched drone that swallowed up all sound except for the lightning and thunder. Through the trees Sarah strained to make out Pepper. He was using his horse as a rain break just as Keene had.

Carefully, she made her way past, picking her way through the trees and the mud. About five hundred yards in front of Pepper, she topped out the appaloosa on a rise.

It was a good vantage to watch for Steele, well hidden by thick pine trees, and despite the heavy curtain of rain, it gave her a direct line of sight up the riverbed.

Anxiously, Sarah waited . . .

She was cold, her wet clothes clinging to her body underneath her slicker. Lightning flashed above her, followed by a heart-stopping roll of thunder. It sounded like the whole mountain was going to come down on top of her. The appaloosa moved about uneasily, agitated by the powerful storm. Remembering what her father use to do, Sarah attempted to calm the big horse by patting its neck and rubbing behind its ears. It did little to settle the frightened horse.

What was she doing out here, Sarah thought to herself? And was she helping Keene or being a hindrance?

The rain was not letting up, if anything, it was getting heavier. Sarah pulled her hood down tighter against her head. She wanted to climb underneath the appaloosa just as Pepper and Keene had done, but she had a better view from the saddle.

For several minutes the lightning and thunder had stopped. Once, Sarah thought she heard the shouts of voices and the sound of riders, and her heart began to pound furiously. She raised up in the stirrups to try and get a better view, but when no riders came she settled back down.

Out of the wet, black night, a bolt of lighting lit up the sky, striking and tearing through one of the nearby trees. The flash of light was blinding and the sound almost deafening. A resounding roll of thunder followed seconds later.

Sarah thought the world was coming to an end. The appaloosa spooked, kicked its front legs up, and bucked Sarah from the saddle. Her back hit the muddy ground and she began to tumble down the incline.

Several times Sarah hit her head, but she was fortunate for the ground had softened from two days of steady rain. She threw out her arm in an attempt to stop her momentum, but the weight of her body snapped it back, breaking it.

Through the confusion and horror she could see a black hole coming towards her, an empty chasm about to swallow her.

It was the mineshaft and Sarah didn't remember hitting the bottom.

With a wave of his hand, Jason Steele drew up his small army at the edge of the Kern River bed. The reservoir was already over capacity, and the amount of water being fed down from the High Sierra, coupled with the constant deluge of rain over the past two days, had turned the Kern back into a mighty river to be feared.

Joe couldn't believe it. "There must be three feet of water in there!"

Steele sloshed his stallion into the middle, followed by the rest of his men. With their heads bent low against the storm, they pushed on. There wasn't far to go now, and soon it would all be over. They would be back in their dry bunks, getting the sleep they could now only wish for.

"Hey, boss!" came a yell from the back of the pack. The group pulled up as one, and the rider who had called out rode his mount up next to Steele. He pointed to a horse standing near the river's edge.

"Awfully far out to be one of ours," Steele reasoned.

"You want to send someone to check it out?" Joe asked.

Steele was not in a patient mood. He had only one thing on his mind and that was getting the Bar MC. He was not about to wait. "No, I don't want to waste time out here."

The heavy veil of rain and the distance made it difficult to make out exactly what kind of horse it was. To Adam, though, it seemed vaguely familiar. "I'll check it out," he volunteered.

Steele nodded. "Fine—but we're not waiting!" Steele waived his hand in the air. "Let's move!" He kicked the stallion and the rest of the men followed their leader, splashing upstream.

Curious, Adam LeFloure led his dun over to the river's edge. Sure enough, his hunch was confirmed. It was Sarah's appaloosa—*and it was saddled.*

His mind lingered on the question: why would Sarah's horse be way out here? She couldn't have possibly ridden out in this rainstorm . . . or could she?

If Sarah had ventured out, she should be by the French Gulch Bridge where Keene was expecting Steele. It gave Adam a disturbing feeling.

Twisting in the saddle, Adam watched the last of Steele's men disappear upstream into the gray wall of rain. He would be of no use to Steele in his assault on the Bar MC, and he was planning to take no part in the raid, anyhow. His interest was, as he told Steele, strictly personal. Sarah had used him and he wanted to be there to witness her downfall. He decided to investigate the appaloosa mystery further.

The pain in Sarah's legs seized her from the moment she came to. She knew instantly they were broken. What Sarah didn't know kept her from going into immediate shock. The cold water pooled to her shoulders obscured the fact her legs were bent behind her like a rag doll tossed into a corner. Her right arm was also broken; however, the pain in her legs was so great she couldn't feel anything else.

The splashing of rain gave off a high-pitched ping as it hit the ground above, before pouring down the incline and into the top of the shaft. The water level was rising rapidly.

Pain knifed through Sarah's body and she fought to stay conscious. She made a vain attempt to get to her feet, but the pain crippled her. Sarah cried out in agony and fell back down. Why hadn't she listened to Keene and gone back to the ranch, she now thought to herself? When would she ever learn to listen?

Sarah was alone and afraid to die. She had been so brave when she rode out to join Keene, but now she was terrified of the darkness. She wasn't as brave as she had believed. She recalled what Keene had said the day before: *Faith is all some people have, and usually they come to find out, it's all they really needed.*

Nothing could save Sarah now except a faith she did not have. How could she believe in something she did not understand? Sarah's father had lived his entire life by that faith, but it was not something learned. His faith came from within. It was a part of him just as was his ability to breathe.

Sarah felt a dull ache in her head now and her vision was becoming blurred. She strained to look up at the top of the hole. It was black except when lightning flashed in the night sky. If the rain didn't stop, she knew she could drown within the hour.

"Help! Please, somebody help me!" Sarah called. Her fearful pleas were swallowed up by the thunder and the rain.

She made another attempted to stand, but the pain intensified causing her to again cry out in agony. She could hardly move and now Sarah looked at death not as a possibility, but a certainty.

The water in the mineshaft continued rising—up to her chin now—and just as there are no atheists in a carriage that has gone off a cliff, neither are there any trapped in a mine shaft, about to drown.

"Oh, God, please don't let me die here!" she sobbed.

Sarah's life unfolded before her. There were so many things about herself she would change—her selfishness for one. All her life she had been scratching and clawing for things that now seemed to have no meaning. Sarah had felt alone most of her life and now she understood why: she never had anything to live her life for. While her father lived his life for his God, his family, his friends, Sarah had lived strictly for herself.

Her every thought, her every decision, had been predicated on how it would effect *her*. Sarah had never been happy this way. It had made for a very lonely and tiring existence.

She had never accepted her father's faith because Sarah wasn't capable of looking outside herself. When one believes they are in control of their life there is no reason for God, for they themselves are the answer. It is only when one loses oneself completely, and looks outward, that faith becomes possible. Sarah had been witness to a handful of miracles in the past week, and yet she could not believe in one of them. Her father had never seen a miracle, and yet he believed in them all his life. Her selfishness had made her blind to miracles, faith, and God.

Now alone in the dark, legs broken, rising water about to drown her, Sarah realized she had never been able to truly help herself. She needed her father's money to get to school, Adam's assistance to get back East, and Keene's daring and courage to help save the ranch from Steele.

Sarah's body shivered from the cold and shock was settling in. She choked on water and had to tip her head back to keep her mouth above the rising pool. Sarah closed her eyes and began to pray. This time, for the very first time in her life, she meant the words when she said them.

"Sarah?"

She stopped her prayer, listening. She thought she had heard her name being called. Thunder boomed and rolled across the valley. No . . . she had only imagined it. She began to cry.

"Sarah, are you out here? Sarah!"

There was no mistaking it this time. It was Adam LeFloure and he was looking for *her*. "Down here!" Sarah shouted. "In the mineshaft!"

Lighting cracked, sending a flash of light piercing through the wet sky. For an instant, she saw Adam staring down at her from the top of the shaft.

"Adam! Get me out of here!" she sobbed. "My legs are broken and I can't move."

"How did you manage to get in there?" Adam said, caution thick in his tone.

"Lightning spooked my horse. Help me! The water is up to my chin!"

Adam fully comprehended the seriousness of her situation, but he was in no hurry. He was troubled by the mystery of it. "What are you doing out in this terrible storm?"

Sarah coughed out water. "We don't have time for this, right now. I'm going to drown!"

"I want to know what you're doing out here," Adam demanded.

Sarah did not reply. She knew Adam was her only hope of survival, but she was also aware that her answer would put Keene and Pepper both at risk. She remained silent, fighting to keep her chin above water.

"Have you ever known someone who drowned, my dear?" Adam said grimly. "It's a very slow and frightening way to die. I would not wish it on my worst enemy."

Thunder called again from the darkness.

"First the lungs fill up with water," Adam went on, "then you begin choking."

Sarah closed her eyes and tried not to listen. She was afraid to hear anymore. All she had to do was tell Adam what he wanted to hear and she would live . . .

She couldn't do it. She was not going to trade her life for Keene's and Pepper's. Something inside her would not let her answer.

"Sarah, I'm not going to ask you again. Is it truly worth dying for?"

Adam could hear Sarah sobbing in the darkness. Her silence told him there was a very good reason she was out in this storm, even though at the moment it made no sense.

She was in the middle of nowhere, miles from the French Gulch Bridge where Keene had said they would be. What could possibly have brought Sarah out this way?

The Dam!

"He's going to blow up the dam, isn't he?" Adam yelled down at Sarah. "You didn't come to my hotel room to beg my forgiveness, you came to set me up!"

"No!" Sarah cried. "I didn't know anything about Keene's plan when I came to see you."

"You liar!"

Adam had found it strange at the time that Keene would be so forthcoming about his plot to blow up the bridge, but it was bait. And he had taken it, just as Sarah had when Adam stepped in front of her that day from the doorway of the hotel.

Steele would believe Adam had double-crossed him, and if Steele lived would kill him for sure.

"I hope you rot in there," Adam said bitterly.

"Adam, please don't leave me here!"

There was no reply . . . and no figure of Adam standing there when lightning again lit up the sky.

Sarah gagged water. For the first time in her life she had done the right thing, and now she would die for it.

Adam plunged the dun back into the river. He whipped the horse, pushing it hard against the strong current. He must catch up to Steele or he would be a hunted man. The rain pounded down, while thunder boomed and lightning cracked all around him. In the distance, Adam could see the pack of riders ahead.

The report of gunfire had drawn Steele and his men up sharply. It was Pepper firing off his warning shots to Keene.

Steele was alarmed. "Where are those shots coming from?" he hollered at Joe.

"Jason, you have to get out of here!" It was Adam riding up fast from the rear.

A bone-chilling explosion erupted upstream!

The ground rolled beneath Steele and his men, and a rushing wind blew down the riverbed. Horses reared and men fell from their saddles. It was the first time Jason Steele had ever experienced pure fear.

"What the hell was that?" Steele shouted, fighting the stallion. A second blast followed seconds later.

It was Joe who saw it first. "Look out!" he shrieked in terror.

The twenty-foot high wave of water came at them with a terrifying roar, uprooting trees and displacing thousand pound boulders in its path. The wall of water slammed into the pack of riders, engulfing them in a furious rush of violent water.

In an instant, Steele and his men were gone.

22

Pepper nudged Sarah gently. "Sarah, wake up. It's all over . . . Sarah?"

Coming slowly out of her deep sleep, Sarah blinked back the bright rays of sunshine streaming through the open window. She sat up focussing, then suddenly grabbed her arm.

She moved it and it did not hurt. She threw back the bed covers, moving her legs frantically in all directions. There was no pain, no broken bones.

"Sarah, what are you doing?"

"Pepper, how did I get here?"

"I don't know what you mean. You were here when I got back."

She explained to Pepper how she had ridden out to help them, and how lightning had spooked her horse.

"I fell down into the mineshaft," she told him. My legs were broken." She felt them again for comfort.

Pepper stood up from the bed. "You must have been dreaming."

"No, Pepper, I was there. I saw you in the trees under your horse. You were having a cigarette." Pepper reacted— he did have a smoke. "Ask Keene, he'll tell you."

At the mention of his name, Sarah watched Pepper's face fall. "He's alright, isn't he?"

Pepper hesitated and right then Sarah knew. "Oh, dear God, no . . ."

"The fuses must've been too short," Pepper speculated. "There was nothing left up there."

Sarah felt her heart stop. "You didn't find him?"

"No, even the roan was gone. Hell, half the mountain's gone."

Sarah perked up. "Then he's still alive. He's probably on his way back to the ranch right now."

Pepper shook his head. "It's been over four hours."

Sarah was quiet, taking it all in. Finally she asked, "What about Steele?"

"Dead—all of 'em." Pepper moved over to the window, looked out, warm sunlight digging at his eyes. "You know, the sun came out almost the minute it was over."

Pepper turned from the window to find Sarah putting on her riding boots. "What are you doing?" he asked, even though he knew the answer.

"I'm going to go find him. He's not dead, Pepper. I won't let him be."

Sarah reached for her hat on the dresser, but it wasn't there. It wasn't on the oak coat tree either, or hanging on the door. Then she remembered losing it in her fall.

It was so real, how could it all have been a dream? But there she was safe in her room, her reflection staring back at her in the mirror.

Sarah hurried out of the room. She didn't have time to look for the hat now. She must go find Keene.

Golden rays of sunshine fanning down through the broken clouds greeted Sarah, upon her arrival at the dam area. A rainbow arced nearby over the Kern River. Sarah never did find a trace of Keene, but she did find her hat. It was resting on its crown beside the black hole of the mineshaft.

Sarah looked out from the stage station up the main street of Canaan Creek. The newly painted town buildings gleamed in the afternoon sun. Wagons and horses moved about the street and the boardwalks were filled with people coming and going. Canaan Creek looked fresh and alive, and there was a spirit of optimism that permeated through the entire valley, down into the roots of the tall grass now growing in the green meadows. Seven months had passed since Jason Steele's defeat in the riverbed.

In the days and weeks following Keene's disappearance, Sarah had refused to believe Keene was dead. Daily she would ride up to the dam area searching for some clue, some sign of his existence. As the days turned into weeks and the weeks into months, her rides became less and less frequent.

Keene was gone, swallowed up in the explosion. Still, Sarah thought of him everyday. Sometimes she would sit for hours watching the front gate of the Bar MC, hoping to see him ride in atop his roan . . . he never did.

Even then, looking up the main street of Canaan Creek, she found herself searching for him. Who was Keene, and how did he know and do the things he did? Sarah resigned herself to the fact she would never know, but that did not mean she would ever stop pondering the question in the deep corners of her mind.

Pepper stepped up beside her. "I look for him, too," he said, knowing what she was thinking. "He reminded me a lot of your father."

Sarah nodded. After a moment she said, "I hate good-byes."

"Ma'am, we're ready to go." It was the driver holding open the coach door.

Sarah wrapped her arms around Pepper, pulling him close like she used to do with her father when she was a little girl. "It's funny—all my life I've wanted to leave this town, and now that it's time, I don't want to go." She dabbed at her tears with the back of her finger. "So much has changed."

"Including you," Pepper said proudly.

Sarah smiled, appreciating the comment. She reached into her leather bag and pulled out the deed to the Bar MC. "I want you to have this, Pepper."

"I can't take that, it belongs to you."

"Then it's mine to give. What am I going to do with a ranch? My father would want you to have it. Don't worry about me, I'll have more money than I'll ever need from some of that land we sold off."

Pepper was deeply moved. "Sarah—"

"Pepper Martin, you take that!" she said, thrusting the deed into his hand.

"I don't know what to say."

"Just promise me you'll come visit a lonely girl at school in Boston once in awhile."

Pepper grinned. "That's a promise I look forward to keeping."

The stage yanked to a start. Sarah leaned out the window, wiping her tears and waving to Pepper until he, along with the false fronts of Canaan Creek, finally disappeared from view.

Through the coach window, Sarah watched in sadness as the Sierra peaks passed by. She was leaving her home and a life she only now realized she loved. This was the day she had dreamed of her entire life, and as it is with most dreams, reality made them into something much different, less perfect.

Alone in the coach, Sarah stretched out to get comfortable. When her baggage was being loaded, she overheard one of the drivers saying she would be the only passenger until the next stop at Indian Wells, about 50 miles away. She would have two hours to be alone with her thoughts.

Sarah wiped away the last of her tears. Opening her purse to put away her handkerchief, she noted the *King James Bible* of her father's that she had tucked away for the ride. Sarah had never read from her father's Bible, but she had brought it with her for comfort for the long journey ahead.

Touching the soft leather cover made Sarah feel close to her father. She placed the Bible in her lap and the pages fell open by themselves to a spot it had been opened to many times before. An underlined passage caught her attention—Exodus 23:20—and she began to read:

*Behold, I send an Angel before thee, to keep thee
in the way, and bring you into the place which I
have prepared.*

*Beware of him, and obey his voice, provoke him
not; for he will not pardon your transgressions; for
my name is in him.*

*But if thou shalt indeed obey his voice, and do all
that I speak; then I will be an enemy unto thine
enemies, and an adversary unto thine adversaries.*

The stagecoach climbed steadily. The team of horses
strained against the leather traces, pulling the coach up
and over Walker's Pass, leaving the Kern River Valley and
the tall Sierra peaks behind.